ONE

MORGAN

CU01507491

Tonight is the night.

I can feel it in my bones, in the way every nerve thrums with electricity. There's a magnetic pull toward something in his pocket, and I know it's a ring.

The ring.

The one I've craved my entire life.

James Whittier is finally going to propose.

We've been together for six months, but who says that's too soon for love? I've lost track of how many dates we've had—surely that means something, right? He must feel what I feel. Must know that I am his forever, just as he is mine.

My heart's practically soaring as we dine at Deckard's, the most exclusive restaurant in the city. It must have taken him forever just to get the reservation, and the bill will easily hit five hundred dollars—an absurd amount for one dinner. James isn't wealthy; he's a plumber who works hard for what he has. Yet here we are, candlelight flickering between us, the soft piano music dancing in the background. It's all so perfect, I can't stop smiling.

I study him from across the table—his gentle features, his callused hands, that tousled dark hair. Those chocolate-brown eyes, warm enough to sink into, spark with something that makes my breath catch. He'll be a wonderful father to the three babies we'll have—two boys and a girl—and we'll live in a house with a wraparound porch and white picket fence. Eventually, I'll be that sweet, bookish old woman with the perfect life, still working at the library because I want to, not because I have to.

I'm aware of how pathetic it might sound, but I can't help it. Love is an intoxicating, exciting dream, and right now, I'm gladly lost in it.

"Morgan?" James's voice snaps me back to reality. The waiter lingers, ready to take our order. I clear my throat and glance at the menu. I have no clue what it says. There aren't even prices listed.

"I'll have what he's having," I say, flashing the kind of smile I hope James finds adorable.

The waiter pours our drinks and disappears. James lifts his glass.

"To the future," he says.

Heat blooms in my cheeks, and I raise my glass to his. "To the future."

It's not long before the food comes—Wagyu steak that melts on my tongue, a decadent chocolate slice more divine than anything I've ever tasted.

When James motions for the check, it arrives tucked in a leather book. He barely glances at it before handing

THE NEWLYWED

ZIA RAYYAN

over his card. He's so calm, so assured, that my pulse flutters with anticipation.

This must be it.

My ring is coming.

Within moments, the bill is paid, and we're stepping out into the crisp night air, streetlights casting a golden haze around us. James guides me along the sidewalk, and I follow without question, heart pounding at the thought of a diamond on my finger.

Truth be told, I thought he might propose inside Deckard's, but maybe he wants a private moment—something that belongs only to us.

He leads me to his truck. We stop, and he turns to me, his gaze settling on my lips before returning to my eyes. My heart nearly bursts. I rise on my toes, certain I'm seconds away from hearing the words I've waited for my whole life.

"Morgan," he says softly.

I bite my lip in excitement. Finally, there'll be someone there to hold me. Someone who'll love me unconditionally, which is all I've ever wanted.

My grin is so wide my cheeks hurt. "Yes?"

He kisses me—long and slow—and my knees go weak, tears welling up in my eyes.

He pulls back, his mouth opening and closing, like he can't quite find the words. My enthusiasm spills over, and I rush into the silence.

"Yes!" I squeal, jumping on my toes. "I will marry you. A thousand times yes!"

But he doesn't move.

He doesn't drop to one knee. He doesn't bring out a ring. He just... stands there.

A flicker of something like guilt crosses his features, and a sick, cold feeling crawls into my stomach.

"James?" I whisper, my voice trembling. "You were going to say something, right?"

He exhales. The sound is empty and hollow. "Morgan, I never said I was proposing."

The words knock the wind out of me. "But— Deckard's, the toast, dinner... I thought..."

I drift off, unable to finish.

His gaze darts anywhere but at me. He doesn't apologize, doesn't offer any explanation beyond a shake of his head.

"You... don't want to marry me? Not now?"

His silence speaks volumes. Panic thrums in my veins. "James, you don't have to propose this second! We can wait!"

He just wrenches open his truck door, climbs inside, and slams it shut. My pulse spikes in desperation to save him, to save the dying dream of a love that'll last *forever*. But the engine roars to life, and I can only stand there helplessly, my dress and heels mocking me in the chilly night.

"James!" I cry, my voice cracking, but he drives off, taillights fading around the corner.

I don't know how long I stand on that sidewalk, shock freezing me in place. It's long enough for the chill to seep into my bones and for my feet to begin aching.

Eventually, I force myself to move, all too aware of my pathetic reflection staring back at me from the shop windows, mascara streaking down my cheeks. Strangers give me sidelong glances as I pass them. But I don't care. I don't have the capacity to.

It's a long bus ride home to my rundown apartment. It leaves me numb, heartbreak having ripped through me like a buzz saw. And despite all that, when I collapse onto the sofa, I check my phone, praying that James has reached out.

Nothing.

A fresh stab of pain slices through me. Why does no one ever choose me? Am I too needy? Too boring? Too ugly?

My gaze drifts to a glossy flyer on the coffee table:

Eden, where love begins at first sight.

The photo shows a couple in a sun-drenched field, gazing at each other, eyes shining with love. I should laugh. No dating? Marrying the moment you meet? It's *ridiculous.*

But still, the thought of a love that's effortless has me holding a breath. If something like that worked out for me, I would never have to worry about being left heartbroken and alone on the curb.

I numbly reach for my phone and pull up Eden's homepage. The website is bright and cheery, full of couples beaming at the camera. Maybe they're stock photos. Maybe they're not. I don't care. I just fill out the form, tears burning my eyes as I admit how desperate I am for a future that I can't seem to get on my own.

Thank you for choosing Eden. We will be in touch.

The automated response glows on my screen. I close my eyes, letting the darkness of the apartment wrap around me. My mind flickers back to James driving away, the sound of his peeling tires driving home the nail of realization that I wasn't worth the proposal I'd so fool-ishly imagined.

I should slow down, think this through. But the hole James left behind *aches*. It's so raw that at this point, I'll do anything to fill it, including marrying someone at first sight.

Maybe that's what it'll take to be loved. Maybe this is how I skip the heartbreak and go straight to "happily ever after." And who knows... if I'm feeling like this, then others could be too, possibly even the perfect man who'll be able to give me that white picket fence dream and those three perfect kids.

Outside, a car door slams in the distance, the sound echoing like a gunshot. I should've taken that as my warning.

Some things are better left as dreams.

TWO
MORGAN

I'm almost late to work the next morning, but not because I've overslept. In truth, I barely slept at all, lying awake until dawn, staring at my phone's blank screen. I half-expected James to call—maybe to say he made a terrible mistake. Or, more realistically, I hoped Eden would send a confirmation email about my application, saying that there was a perfect man out there for me.

Of course, there was nothing. Not a word from either. And really, why should there be? The application was only submitted that same night, and as for James... well, why would he call me after leaving me stranded on the curb like that?

A man doesn't do that unless he's well and truly done with you.

And yet, I hoped.

It's not lost on me how pathetic and desperate that makes me. But I tell myself this: there's not a soul alive who hasn't felt this kind of craving. At least, that's what I want to believe.

By the time I unlock the glass doors of the library where I work, my eyes feel grainy and swollen from crying. But I paste on a bright smile for the handful of early-bird patrons waiting outside. As soon as I flip the "Closed" sign to "Open," they shuffle in with their usual greetings.

I slip behind the circulation desk, my heels clicking softly on the tiled floor. The space is familiar—wooden counters, the hum of computers a decade behind modern tech, and the faint beep each time someone scans a library card. Usually, the comfort of routine helps me find my center, but now all I can think about is how there seem to be so many people checking out romance books— stories so unlike my own, where no happy ending seems to be on the horizon.

Tiana appears beside me, setting down a box of newly arrived paperbacks. She's wearing a bright yellow cardigan that pops against her tanned skin, and I can't help noticing how awake she looks, as if she actually got some sleep.

"Morning," she says, side-eyeing me with a concerned frown. "You okay? You seem... off."

"Just tired," I say. I click open our library software, scanning the spines of returned books. My fingers tremble on the keys, and I know Tiana doesn't miss it.

"I'm guessing last night didn't go like you wanted it to?"

My shoulders stiffen, and I force myself to meet her eyes. "He, um... kind of..." My throat constricts, and that sick wave of embarrassment heats my cheeks. "We broke up."

Her eyes flood with sympathy and she uncharacteristically wraps her arms around me. "Oh, Morgan. I'm sorry. That's rough. Especially since you... well, you seemed to really like him."

The words scramble out before I can stop them. "I thought he was going to propose, Tiana." My cheeks burn hotter. I hate how desperate I sound. "We went to Deckard's last night, and everything felt so perfect, right up until he left me on the sidewalk. He just... drove away. Didn't even tell me why."

Her eyes go wide. "Wow. That's... wow."

I let out a laugh that sounds more like a wounded bark. "I thought we were in love."

She squeezes my arm. "I know it doesn't help, but sometimes men freak out when things get serious. Maybe... maybe he just got scared off? Austin was like that when he was trying to propose to me."

"You didn't see him. He was... I don't know." I push away the lump in my throat. I shake my head and try to distract myself, as though scanning barcodes might somehow scan the pain out of me. "Something in me tells me that James isn't coming back."

She doesn't say anything. What can you say?

"I'm not going to sit around and mope though," I say, despite the fact that I may have done exactly that all night. "I already applied for something that might help me move on."

Tiana's eyebrows lift. "What kind of something?"

I hesitate, my tongue darting across my lips. A flicker of doubt flutters in my chest, but I shove it down. "It's called Eden. Have you heard of them?"

She shakes her head.

A customer steps up, an old woman who wanted some help finding a book she'd heard about. When the woman is gone with her "spicy" novel, Tiana looks at me.

"So... Eden?" she asks.

I look around to make sure no other customers are coming. The last thing I want is for anybody to overhear just how desperate for love I am.

"It's a matchmaking service. They uh... well, they match you to a perfect man and help you skip all the heartbreak."

She draws back. "Skip the heartbreak?"

"Yeah." I bite my lip. "It's a marriage-at-first-sight service."

She starts cackling, the sound of her voice disrupting the silence. More than a few people walking around with books in their hands stop to look our way.

But when Tiana sees the serious look on my face, her laughter dies in her chest and her eyes fill with horror. "You're serious."

"I am. I'm tired of messing around with these dating apps. You know just how bad they can be. How many people are just looking to get laid, or are wanting to take their sweet time being serious?" I shake my head, reaching for another book on the endless stack to scan. "This is good. This is... real."

"But what? How does that even work?"

"I'm not too sure. The website didn't say much. But there's an interview."

Tiana stares at me for a long moment, and in a deadpan voice, repeats after me, "There's an interview."

I nod.

She draws a deep breath, then sighs. "Morgan, this is a bad idea."

"Why?"

"Because it sounds too good to be true. How can you honestly expect them—people who don't even know you—to find you the perfect man?"

"They're experts. It's supposed to be an elite service."

Tiana leans back against the counter and crosses her arms. "You know that real relationships are messy, right? You can't just do something like this and expect a fairy-tale ending. Love takes work—two people getting to know each other's flaws and insecurities, deciding they're worth sticking around for anyway."

My jaw tightens, and I look down at the chipped polish on my nails. "I know that. But I don't have a great track record with love, okay? I'm always the one who ends up blindsided, and forgive me if I don't want to end up alone on the side of the road with my heart in pieces again."

Her expression softens, and she rounds the counter to stand right next to me. "Listen, I know what you're going through. I'm just saying... be careful, okay? It feels like there's got to be a catch to this."

"I appreciate the concern," I manage, offering a tight smile. "But I've already signed up, so I'm going to follow through. Who knows? It might actually work."

She holds my gaze for another beat, then nods. "Okay," she says quietly, stepping back to gather a stack of returned magazines. "But if something feels off... promise me you won't ignore it."

"I promise."

She disappears into a far aisle, the sound of her footsteps swallowed by the hush of the library. As the clock inches toward ten, the library becomes busier—mothers with toddlers in tow, elderly patrons who use the public computers, students on break. It's a steady hum of life that distracts me from the raw ache in my chest. But every so often, I catch myself checking my phone screen.

And each time, I see nothing.

Until—

My phone starts to ring, and a name flashes across the screen.

Eden.

I practically vault away from the checkout counter, ignoring the exasperated looks of patrons coming to stand in line. My heart drums against my chest, so loud I swear everyone in the library can hear it. But at this moment, I can't bring myself to care.

"Hello?" I say, my voice trembling with barely contained excitement.

A smooth, reassuring voice responds on the other end. "Hello, Morgan. I'm Dexter, your dedicated Eden representative. I understand you're interested in our service."

My breath catches. "Right, yes," I manage, trying to steady my voice. "I'm... I'm very interested."

I can almost picture Dexter smiling. "Excellent. Before we go further, may I ask why you're looking into Eden? We like to ensure every participant is fully committed. I'm sure you understand."

I nod, even though he can't see me, clinging to the phone like it's a lifeline. And in a sad sort of way, it *is*.

"Of course. I, um... I just went through a bad breakup. Honestly, I thought he was going to propose. Turns out he wasn't even close to that." The words tumble out in a rush, and I release a shaky breath. "Anyway, I'm tired of the games—of hoping and being disappointed. I just want something real and permanent. Your site mentioned love at first sight, without the heartbreak... that's exactly what I need."

"I see. Thank you for sharing. Eden can indeed match you with someone who values commitment just as strongly as you do."

Music to my ears.

"Are you available for an in-depth interview soon? We do require these be done in person, so that we can gather everything we need to get you the best possible match."

"Yes," I say without hesitation. But then I wince, and worry creeps into my voice. "Sorry, I just realized you said the interview would have to be in person? Where are you located?"

Dexter chuckles from the other side of the phone, "Don't be worried, Morgan. We come to you to conduct the interview."

I blink. "Oh, you do?"

"We stick by our mission. We believe that love comes to you."

The corner of my lips creeps upward into a smile, and I start to feel the pieces of my shattered heart coming back together. A little silly, I know, given that James broke up with me just late last night. But the prospect of all this was exciting.

Tiana returns to the counter and sees the line of customers waiting. She flashes me a look of annoyance, but is kind enough to handle them herself while I'm on the phone.

"That's great," I say, aware that I need to get back to work. "So when should we do this?"

I hear the click of a keyboard in the background, and Dexter offers me a few dates. We schedule something in, and Dexter wraps up the call with the kind of polished politeness you'd expect from a first-class concierge.

A tiny spark of hope flares in the emptiness James left behind. Maybe, just *maybe*, Eden really can offer me what I've been searching for all along.

Unable to wipe the grin off my face, I take my place back at the counter. My heart is still pounding in excitement, because right now, I'm choosing to believe in that sliver of possibility.

Maybe I am foolish, maybe I am desperate—but I'm also not ready to give up on the idea that this time, it was my turn for a happy ending.

And I'd do anything to have it.

THREE
MORGAN

A few days crawl by before I find myself sitting with Dexter in the library's cramped conference room, a windowless space tucked behind the archives. The distant hum of the ventilation system only makes the hush seem louder.

It's not the ideal spot for an interview, but I couldn't think of anywhere better—a bustling coffee shop would've been too public for something like this, and my apartment felt too personal. I don't want Dexter to see how bare and lonely my life really is. I'd rather he see me as someone who has it together, someone ready for the next big step.

Because the last thing a man wants to marry is a miserable wreck.

Dexter sits across the table, posture ruler-straight, a sleek black folder open before him. He's dressed in an immaculate suit that looks so expensive I find myself wondering how much a match specialist at Eden must earn.

With one fluid motion, he clicks his pen and leans forward. "All right, shall we begin?"

I inhale, trying to steady the twist in my stomach. Before leaving my desk, I kept repeating the same mantra in my head: You are good. You are beautiful. You are worthy of love. You deserve this.

"Yes," I manage, folding my hands in my lap to keep them from trembling.

"Excellent." Dexter glances at his notes, then meets my eyes. "As we discussed, Eden uses a thorough personal interview to gather information about you—your psyche, habits, preferences, and any past experiences that might impact a long-term commitment. I want to remind you: everything is confidential."

He lifts a finger, as though suddenly recalling an important detail. Sliding a small black briefcase from under the table, he sets it between us and flips it open.

"You'll be subject to a polygraph throughout this interview," he says, removing a device that looks like something straight out of a police drama. "We go to extraordinary lengths to ensure our clients are honest, committed, and accurately matched. It will only benefit you."

I stare at the machine, feeling a ripple of uncertainty. "A polygraph?"

"It's an advanced model," he assures me. "It monitors subtle changes in voice, heart rate, and body language. Think of it as a safeguard that ensures you're paired with someone truly compatible. That can't happen if one party isn't entirely truthful."

I'm hesitant, but eventually I nod, swallowing hard.

After all, people lie every day on dating apps—about their age, their photos, their finances. At least Eden is being transparent about verifying the truth. I'm an honest person. I have nothing to hide. Someone else might, though.

Dexter clips the sensors to my fingertips and secures a thin band around my arm. It's awkward—every shift in my seat rustles the wires—but I push back the flutter of nerves, reminding myself why I'm here.

Once he's satisfied everything is in place, he settles back in his chair and consults a page in his folder. "Let's start with your upbringing. You mentioned in your application that you have no immediate or extended family ties. Is that correct?"

My mouth parts, but I pause, unsure of how to phrase my response. Anxiety flutters in my chest as I glance at the blinking polygraph device.

His gaze flicks up. "Is there a problem?"

"Should I just answer yes or no?"

A faint smile tugs at his lips. "Our system is quite advanced. You can speak normally. I'll ask for clarification if needed."

"Oh, okay. Then... yes, it's true. My parents passed away when I was young, and I'm an only child."

He flips to another sheet. "Any extended relatives— grandparents, uncles, aunts? Even distant cousins?"

I shake my head, then remember to speak aloud. "No. None."

His eyes stray briefly to the polygraph's readings. "Understood. Who would you say is closest to you in life right now?"

A lump forms in my throat. I hate saying it, but I can't lie. "No one, really. I've moved around a lot, so I never formed lasting friendships. My coworker Tiana is the only person I talk to regularly, and even that's just... casual."

"So, objectively, you are alone."

I bristle at his blunt phrasing, but manage a nod. "Yes."

He offers me a look that I suppose is meant to be sympathetic. "Thank you for your honesty. These are the kinds of details we need, because your perfect match might come with a supportive family who will welcome you wholeheartedly. That's often crucial for someone in your position."

My chest tightens at the thought. A mother-in-law who dotes on me. A father-in-law who sees me as one of his own. Siblings to share jokes and holidays and inside stories. The idea sends a wave of warmth through me, pushing aside the mild discomfort I feel over being hooked to a lie detector.

"That... that would be nice," I admit.

Dexter scribbles something in his folder. "Next question: how has this loneliness shaped your sense of belonging? Do you fear letting others close?"

"I guess it's made me clingy," I say quietly. "If I find someone worth loving, I'll do anything to keep them from leaving. I mean *anything*."

He nods, his pen gliding across the page in neat, deliberate strokes. "And how did that play out with your ex-boyfriend, James?"

A small pang pierces my chest. I don't remember mentioning him on the application. Did I?

"He left anyway," I say softly. "I thought that being sweet and attentive would keep him, but... it wasn't enough."

Dexter's detached hum makes the words sound more clinical than they should. I force myself to take a calming breath, reminding myself that I won't have to repeat these answers once I'm finally matched and married. The man I marry will already know all this—he'll love me for it.

Dexter flips to a new page. "Some general lifestyle preferences... Favorite form of exercise?"

"I like long walks. Hate running, but I don't mind biking."

"Favorite place?"

"My bed," I say, then flush at how that sounds.

After a moment of scanning more notes, he levels his gaze at me. "Are you sexually active?"

The question knocks the air from my lungs. "What?"

"Or are you a virgin?"

"Why're you asking me that?"

"It's an important aspect of compatibility," he says calmly, waiting.

Heat rushes to my cheeks. I glance at the machine, conscious that any hesitation might be noted. "Yes... I am a virgin."

His brow lifts. "Have you engaged in *any* form of sexual activity?"

I exhale, shaky. "No."

He jots this down. "How would you describe your libido?"

A bubble of disbelief escapes as a nervous laugh. "You're kidding me, right?"

He taps a pen against his folder. "Intimacy is often the cornerstone of a strong marriage. We can skip this if you're uncomfortable, but we can't promise an ideal match without full disclosure."

My chest tightens as I picture another lonely night in my apartment, James's memory haunting me. I suck in a breath. "Fine. I... I'd say I have a high libido."

His gaze flickers over me, and I can't read his expression. It makes my pulse stutter uncomfortably. He notices. I see his eyes drift to the polygraph's readings.

"Moving on to finances. Are you in ownership of any property or hold substantial assets like stocks or crypto?"

A rueful laugh escapes me. "No. Just student loans, credit card debt, the usual. Librarians don't make much money."

"I see."

My shoulders tense, though I can't figure out why.

"Children—do you want them?"

"Yes," I answer immediately, thinking again of that picket fence dream. "At least three. Eventually."

He lifts his gaze from the folder. "Would you compromise if your match wanted fewer—or none at all?"

My heart constricts. The notion of letting that dream slip away stings. But losing a potential partner stings worse.

"I'd be open to discussing it. But ideally... yes, I want them."

Dexter sets the pen down and meets my eyes. "Last question, Morgan. If your perfect partner asked you to uproot your entire life—move across the country or over-seas—would you do it? No questions asked?"

I can feel my pulse in my ears, and the conference room walls feel like they're closing in a fraction. The safest answer would be, 'We'll discuss it.' But I recall the Eden motto, the guarantee of skipping heartbreak if I commit wholeheartedly.

"Yes," I whisper, my voice shaky. "I'd do it in a heartbeat."

Dexter's lips curve into a measured smile. "That's wonderful, Morgan. Thank you for being so forthcoming." He neatly unhooks me from the polygraph, collects his notes, and rises. "I'll finalize these and forward them to my colleagues. We should have a decision for you within the week."

I nod, feeling like my mouth is full of sand. "Thank you."

He heads to the door, pressing a hand to the handle. But something gnaws at me.

"Wait," I blurt.

Dexter pauses, glancing back.

"You said 'a decision.' I thought I was already accepted?"

"You are. The 'decision' refers to selecting a perfect match. Once we've done that, the next steps will be arranged—swiftly." A hint of a smile flickers at the corner of his mouth. "By this time next week, you could be married."

My mind spins at the word.

"Married," I echo.

He inclines his head. "We'll be in touch soon, Morgan."

Then, with that same polite, measured confidence, he slips into the hallway and is gone.

I stay there for a long moment, the fluorescent lights humming faintly above me. My heartbeat thuds against my ribs. That was easily the most invasive round of questions I've ever faced.

But it's for a good reason, I remind myself. Eden needs this information if they're truly going to find me the perfect man. Isn't that what I've been longing for? A guarantee of love and commitment—a life free of the heartbreak James left behind?

Still, a knot of unease tightens in my stomach as I flick off the light and step into the corridor. It isn't just the questions that linger—it's the fact that not once did Dexter mention a price.

And if there's one thing I know about things without a price tag...

They always cost more than you can afford.

FOUR

MORGAN

The following days are an odd mixture of tension and numbness. I keep expecting my phone to ring at random moments—on the bus, at the library, in the grocery store. Every time it chimes, my heart leaps, only to deflate when it's just a spam text or my phone reminding me about upcoming bills.

I'm hardly sleeping, too excited by the possibility of a perfect match. It sounds like a fairy tale, and I can't stop thinking about what kind of man would want to build a life with me.

No games, no heartbreak, no leaving me on the sidewalk in my best dress with tears rolling down my face.

But as the days pass with increasing silence, the doubts start to creep in. Maybe the polygraph revealed something they didn't like. Maybe I seemed too desperate, too lonely. Too messed up. It gets to where every time I look in the mirror, that's all I can see. The pathetic, embarrassing, desperate woman that I am.

The following Wednesday morning, I'm so on edge

that I nearly snap at a teenager trying to check out a stack of adult thrillers without a proper library card. The poor kid flinches, and I have to apologize over and over, cheeks burning with embarrassment. Tiana gives me a sharp look from across the desk, clearly worried.

At lunch, I lock myself in the staff bathroom and breathe—in for four, hold for four, out for four. It's a trick I read about in some self-help book one day while scanning it in. But it doesn't help much.

My phone remains silent, perched on the edge of the sink. I consider texting Eden's main contact number. Would that make me look unhinged? Possibly. But if they told me a decision would come within a week, and well... we're pretty much there.

So why hasn't Dexter called?

My phone suddenly rings, startling me so badly I almost drop it in the sink. The screen flashes with Eden's name. I scramble to answer it, pressing the phone so tightly to my ear it aches.

This time, I look in the mirror and spot the fear in the green eyes staring back at me.

"Hello?" I manage, voice trembling.

"Hello, Morgan," Dexter's familiar tone replies, smooth and calm. "How are you today?"

"I'm... I'm fine," I stammer. "I was starting to wonder if maybe I'd ever hear from you again. Thought maybe I failed your interview or something."

He chuckles softly. "I assure you, Eden doesn't operate on a pass-fail system. We've just been finalizing some crucial details for your match."

My breath catches. "So, you found someone?"

A short pause. "We have, indeed. Someone who meets your preferences in every category, from emotional needs to lifestyle compatibility. A truly perfect man for you. I believe you'll be very pleased."

I press a palm to my chest, trying to steady my breath. There's someone out there for me. "Oh, my God. Okay, yes, that's great. That's amazing! What's his name? What's he look like? Is he—"

"Take a deep breath, Morgan," he says, cutting through my words.

"Sorry," I laugh, my hands shaking and my jaw chattering with excitement. "I'm just... you know."

"Excited. You have a very good reason to be. This is one of the best men to come through our program."

"He is?" I practically melt in front of the mirror. I let out a long breath. "What happens next?"

"Now, we move forward with the next steps, introducing you to your perfect match at the altar. Our main goal at Eden is ensuring your immediate and lasting happiness. Thus, we'd like to expedite the process. We're prepared to arrange the ceremony at our private retreat if you're available to travel soon."

My head spins. "Uh... how soon?"

Dexter's tone remains unfailingly polite. "Within the next forty-eight hours."

"What?" My voice echoes in the tiled bathroom. "That's... that's really fast."

"As we mentioned, our service is built on skipping the messy parts and going straight to a committed relationship." He pauses. "If you're uncomfortable with the timeframe, we can discuss alternatives. However, your match is eagerly awaiting the opportunity to meet you. And we do find that moving quickly helps preserve the excitement—and the certainty—of the match."

I close my eyes, Tiana's warnings ringing through my head like a distant alarm. Is this entirely insane? Absolutely. But at the same time, my mind conjures images of that white picket fence, the husband who never leaves, the family dinners I've only seen in movies. Isn't this what I wanted?

The words spill out before I can stop myself. "Yes. I can go."

"Excellent," Dexter replies. "I'll email your flight itinerary and retreat details. We'll handle all accommodations, including attire, meals, and lodging. Please note that we do ask for discretion—Eden prides itself on offering a private experience for both parties."

I swallow hard. "Discretion. Right."

"Excellent, we'll be seeing you soon, Morgan."

"Wait!"

"Yes?"

"What about a wedding dress? Don't I need to get one?"

"As I mentioned, all your attire has been covered."

I blink. "You're covering my wedding dress?"

"Yes, that's correct."

"Oh. Well, what if I don't like the dress?"

"I very much doubt that will be the case, Morgan. Should you be displeased with it, though, please inform me and we'll make whatever arrangements necessary."

I start to hear the tension in his voice, the impatience and annoyance. So I let loose a shaky breath and force myself to relax. What am I being so difficult for? Not only were they paying for everything, they'd found me the one thing that mattered most.

A perfect man.

"Thank you, Dexter. Words can't really express how excited I am. Nervous, yes, but excited!" I bite my lip, debating on my next question, not wanting to be any more bothersome that I've been already. But I can't help myself. "Can you tell me his name?"

"I could, but I think it'd mean more coming from him. You're only two days out now, Morgan, from the rest of your life. We'll see you soon."

The call ends, and I stare at my phone. A private experience at a resort with a man I've never met. I didn't even know his name.

It sounds like a delirious fantasy—and maybe it is.

I stare at my phone for what feels like forever, frozen in the library's staff bathroom. My reflection in the mirror looks exactly how I feel—wide-eyed, breathless, teetering between terror and exhilaration. This is happening. I'm really going to leave everything behind in two days to marry a stranger at some secret resort.

I tug open the bathroom door and step out into the hallway, my entire body buzzing with adrenaline and my skin tingling. Before I can collect myself, Tiana nearly runs into me.

"Whoa, you okay?" she asks.

I swallow. "I need to talk to you. I'm going to need a leave of absence."

Her eyebrows shoot up. "For how long?"

"I don't know."

"Morgan, what's going on?"

"Eden found me a match. I'm headed to a private retreat for the wedding ceremony. Tomorrow."

She stares at me, disbelief washing over her face. "You're actually marrying a stranger? Just like that?"

"This is what I've been waiting for—someone who won't leave, who wants commitment. Someone who's Eden guaranteed."

"Guaranteed?" She shakes her head. "Morgan—"

"Please," I interrupt. "Don't try to talk me out of it. I've waited my whole life for someone to choose me. Just trust me?"

She runs a hand over her forehead. "Fine. Promise me if something feels off, you'll get out of there immediately."

"I promise."

"I'll cover your hours and tell Margaret it's a family emergency." She sets a hand on my shoulder. "I think this is crazy, but I hope you find what you're looking for."

My throat thickens. I swallow the emotions threatening to spill over and offer a tentative smile.

"Me too."

FIVE
MORGAN

What happens next is nothing short of a fairy tale.

I stuff my few vacation-worthy outfits into a suitcase —my bikini, my cutest dresses, and the only pair of sandals I own that don't look like they've been through a war—then drag it to the curb outside my apartment. I expect to haul it onto a bus, maybe fight off a roach or two, and pray no one sits too close.

But then a black Rolls-Royce glides to a stop in front of me.

I freeze, gripping the handle of my suitcase like I might be hallucinating. The car is easily the nicest thing I've ever seen outside of the movies. For a second, I wonder if there's been a mistake, if maybe some influencer is doing a segment on where the poor live and I'm about to get yelled at for standing too close to their car.

But then the driver—an older man in a crisp suit— steps out, rounds the car, and opens the door for me, like I'm royalty.

A slow, giddy grin spreads across my face. I tuck my nerves into my back pocket and step inside.

The leather seats are butter-soft. A crystal glass of wine waits in the cupholder, condensation still clinging to the rim like it was poured just moments ago. This is already a thousand times better than cramming into a sweaty bus seat, and I haven't even left my neighborhood yet.

As the car hums to life and pulls away from the curb, I glance out the tinted window, watching the familiar streets pass by in a blur. A nervous, excited energy flutters through me.

This is real. This is happening.

But as the minutes stretch, something tugs at my mind, just enough to tighten my stomach.

I don't recognize the route we're taking.

I hesitate before speaking, not wanting to sound ungrateful, but finally, I clear my throat. "Um... we're going to the airport, right?"

The driver meets my gaze in the rearview mirror and offers a polite smile. "Of course, ma'am."

Except it's not my airport.

The Rolls-Royce glides straight through a security gate stopping in front of a private jet.

I stare.

A private jet? For me?

This must be some kind of mistake. Maybe there was a miscommunication. I thought I'd be taken to a normal flight, with normal people, squeezed between someone's crying toddler and a guy who refuses to use deodorant.

But no. They usher me forward like this is completely

routine, the stairs lined in gold trim. Inside, the jet is empty. No one else in sight. A thick, plush blanket is draped over my seat—nicer than anything I own, softer than I'd ever imagine.

I sink into the chair, inhaling the faint scent of something expensive, something clean and new, and let my eyes drift toward the window. I should've asked more questions, but a numb thrill courses through me.

Marriage first. Questions later.

The thought is ridiculous, but a bubble of laughter escapes my lips anyway, loosening the last of the tension in my shoulders.

What's the worst that could happen?

A flight attendant—because of course there's a flight attendant—approaches with a warm smile and tucks the blanket around me, her movements gentle, practiced. "Would you like anything before takeoff, ma'am?"

I shake my head. As the engines hum to life and the world outside the window begins to blur, I close my eyes and let the sunlight warm my face.

Before I know it, I'm asleep, dreaming of a faceless, perfect man waiting for me at the altar. I can feel the warmth of his hands over mine, and the sweetness of his breath on my face, like he'd just eaten cherries and strawberries.

And when I wake up, a smile spreads across my face. Not because of the man in my dream or the fact that we've arrived at the resort, according to the polite announcement of the flight attendant, but because for once, James was nothing but a distant, hazy fog.

Dexter waits for me at the bottom of the stairs, still

dressed in his perfectly tailored suit with his hands interlaced in front of him. But I barely notice him.

Because past him—stretching endlessly like a vision stolen out of a travel magazine—is the most breathtaking resort I've ever seen.

The beach is flawless. The kind of perfection that doesn't seem real, where the sand is smooth and untouched, and the water laps at the shore in a gentle rhythm. Each room has its own private infinity pool, turquoise water spilling so seamlessly it looks like it merges with the horizon. I realize every room is angled to catch both sunrise and sunset, with greenery spilling in and around the architecture.

Then there's the smell.

The crisp, salty ocean breeze intertwines with something warm and mouthwatering drifting from the central building—grilled meat, fresh bread, maybe something sweet. My breath catches, my eyes flutter shut, and before I can stop myself, a soft, involuntary moan of delight slips past my lips.

I can't even begin to fathom what this place costs per night.

"I hope it's to your liking, Morgan?"

Dexter's voice pulls me from my daze, and I blink, realizing I was probably standing there with my mouth open, seconds away from drooling. Heat creeps into my cheeks, but he only looks politely amused.

I let out a breathless laugh, shaking my head in disbelief. "It's... absolutely stunning."

"Good," he says smoothly. "Now, if you'll come with me, we have a busy day ahead."

As I follow him, I watch my bag being lifted and carried away like it's priceless cargo. Which is funny, considering I nearly broke my back hauling it down my apartment stairs this morning.

We reach a sleek little car waiting near the runway, and once we're seated, Dexter outlines the day's events.

"We'll take you straight to your fitting to ensure your dress is perfectly comfortable. From there, we'll go through the complements—jewelry, shoes, your bag. You'll also receive a selection of clothing for the resort, custom-fitted based on your measurements."

I nod slowly, but my brain is still reeling, struggling to process everything. It feels like I've stepped into someone else's life—someone born into privilege, untouched by heartbreak or finances or anything real.

New clothes. Custom-fitted. A wardrobe waiting for me before nightfall.

How is any of this real?

Dexter continues, entirely unfazed by my stunned silence. "Those items will be delivered to your room before the evening, along with the contents of your bags. Of course, I doubt you'll have much need for them."

His tone is light, but something about his words makes my stomach tighten. My fingers flex against my lap. "Why not?"

He smiles, indulgent. "Because you'll be focused on other things."

"Other things?"

"Your perfect man, Morgan."

My brain stalls. Like an old engine, it sputters to life far too late. "Wait... I'm getting married *today*?"

Dexter chuckles like I just said something adorable. "Of course. Did you think it'd be delayed?"

I blink. My mouth opens, but no words come out.

Today.

"But... my makeup isn't right," I stutter. My stomach rumbles, and suddenly I want to stress eat as every anxiety flares in my head. What if my perfect man takes one look and decides I'm not worth the trouble? Being refused at the altar, in a place like this, might kill me.

Dexter rests a hand on my shoulder in a comforting manner. "You're worried. I understand. But do you have faith in Eden?"

I look up at him. It takes me a moment to respond, but eventually, I whisper, "I do."

"Then trust we've done our due diligence. You have nothing to worry about."

"Not even my dress?"

"Not even that," Dexter says, and the certainty in his voice sends a ripple down my spine.

The car slows as we arrive. Without thinking, I reach for the door handles, but Dexter's voice gives me pause.

"One moment, Morgan," he says. "There *is* one last thing I must ask of you before we continue."

"What is it?"

He smiles almost apologetically as he holds his hand out. "Your phone."

I blink. "My phone? What do you need that for?"

"Eden has gone to great lengths to ensure that you have the perfect match, and that you'll be set to have a successful marriage beyond this resort. But we have found that links to the world beyond this can be a detriment to our matches, particularly in this early stage."

"So you want my phone? I can just turn it off, tuck it away."

"I wish I could allow it, but unfortunately, temptation draws even the best of us. It is a policy of Eden's to collect all personal devices upon arrival."

I glance down my phone in worry. What if I need to call someone? The thought is laughable, because I didn't really have anyone to call, besides Tiana. And even with her, it's not like we were close.

"Don't worry, Morgan. We'll ensure that you and your husband both receive your devices back before you depart the resort."

Husband.

I let out a sigh and pass my phone to Dexter. He *was* right. I'd seen it a million times in the library, when a wife wanted to talk about certain books with her husband only to find him glued to the screen.

Addiction to our screens was an illness that hardly anybody recognized these days. But maybe that's because we were all affected by it. Even me.

Dexter takes my phone and slides it into a ziplock bag and tucks it away. Then he ushers me out of the car and into a suite so lavish I almost forget how to breathe, let alone worry about my phone. Floor-to-ceiling mirrors gleam beneath the glow of chandeliers, while rows of pristine white gowns line the walls. But there's only one that matters.

The dress.

It's in the center of the room, bathed in a soft, flattering light. It isn't the ballgown I might've pictured, but rather a mermaid silhouette, with a sleek bodice that hugs my waist. Delicate lace embroidery drapes like ivy over the fabric, and below the hips, the gown flares in layers of chiffon that pool at the feet like sea foam.

I'm not sure I could have dreamed up anything like this on my own. It's the perfect dress, clearly meant for the perfect bride.

A consultant steps forward with a warm but professional smile, measuring tape draped around her neck, a pin cushion strapped to her wrist. She leads me behind a partition where a silky robe waits. My old clothes vanish, snatched away by hands so quick I barely see them.

When I step into the dress, it molds to me flawlessly.

Like it was made for me. Like it already knew me.

I lift my gaze to the mirror, and my breath catches in my throat.

I don't recognize the woman staring back at me.

She's beautiful. Ethereal. A woman worthy of a fairy tale.

Even Dexter gives me a nod of approval.

At the consultant's soft instruction, I turn, the train sweeping behind me. The motion is effortless, but something thick and unsteady rises in my throat. I blink away tears. No crying. No puffy eyes.

Even if I only found out I was getting married an hour ago.

"Jewelry next," the consultant murmurs, and Dexter steps forward, a velvet case balanced in his hands.

Inside is a delicate chain, spun silver with a diamond

so bright it could've fallen from the stars. A pair of matching earrings gleam beside it.

"Do you remember Eden's motto, Morgan?" Dexter asks.

I meet his eyes. "Love comes to me."

"That's right," he says, smiling with a twinkle in his eye.

I don't ask how they knew exactly what I'd like. Eden knows. They've known all along.

Hands move swiftly, fastening the clasp at my nape, sliding the earrings into place, dusting a final sweep of blush across my cheeks. I barely whisper a "thank you" before I'm led away again—down a corridor lined with flickering lanterns and vases overflowing with white roses. My pulse thuds a steady chant: this is real, this is real, this is real.

We arrive at a set of grand double doors, their gold handles gleaming under the waning daylight.

Dexter rests a hand at my back, a gentle, guiding pressure. "He's waiting just beyond these doors."

My fingers tighten around the bouquet of roses an attendant hands me. Classic. Beautiful. Pure.

This is already more than I ever imagined when I filled in that online application. No expense spared, no detail overlooked. They've given me the kind of fantasy I never thought I'd get, and I'd happily go into debt with Eden for the rest of my life if it means getting a love that won't abandon me.

But a tremor works its way through me as Dexter's words sink in.

He's waiting for me.

The man I'm supposed to love.

The man who's supposed to love me.

Dexter leans in, his voice soft under the rising swell of music beyond the doors. "Don't worry, Morgan. Eden never makes mistakes."

I force a wobbly smile, my breath thin in my chest.

Because on the other side of these doors is everything I've been promised.

All I have to do is step through.

The doors sweep open, and the music rushes in—soft, romantic, something out of a dream. My heart stutters, every nerve in my body wound tight.

I take one last breath.

I should have savored it.

SIX

MORGAN

I take the first step forward onto the red velvet carpet, then the second. I can feel *his* gaze on me, and my pulse hammers against my ribs. I don't dare look up. Not yet.

What if I meet the wrong eyes? Some goth-obsessed man with a neckbeard who thinks he owns me now? Or worse—what if I look up and see disappointment flicker across his face before he schools it into something polite?

The thought makes my stomach lurch, and for a terrifying second, I stumble. My ankle wobbles, but I catch myself just in time. I suck in a breath, too sharp, too shallow. Black dots swim at the edges of my vision.

Do I trust Eden?

My gaze flickers over the room, realizing there's nobody else in the wedding hall except the officiant. I can feel him waiting too, perhaps more patiently than my perfect man. I imagine he's been through this before, day after day with Eden. He's probably seen people turn away out of pure fear of the unknown, who turned their backs against this seemingly airbrushed reality. But I can't bring myself to do that. As much as I don't want to admit it, I *need* this.

I need him.

So why does my skin crawl?

Slowly, hesitantly, I lift my gaze.

Shoes.

Polished black leather, expensive but not flashy. My eyes trail upward, over long legs wrapped in navy slacks—subtle, tailored, expensive in a way that whispers rather than shouts. His hands rest one over the other, a Rolex winking on his wrist.

I don't know why it's his hands that make my breath catch. Maybe it's the veins, the dusting of hair, the quiet strength in them. Hands that could be gentle. Hands that could break things.

My pulse skitters.

I take in his broad chest, the fit of his suit, the sharp, clean jawline that hints at power. And then—

His eyes.

My breath catches, stolen in an instant. A jolt of something electric snaps through me, drowning out everything I thought I knew about love, about attraction, about fate.

I don't know his name. I don't know his voice. I don't know if that mouth will ever curve into a smile meant just for me.

But I know this:

He is the one.

The perfect man, capable of the kind of love that

should not—cannot—be real. And yet, as he looks at me, something inside me screams.

Run.

SEVEN

HENRY

She is absolutely perfect.

I know it the moment she nearly stumbles, her body jolting with uncertainty before she catches herself. The way her eyes flick up, the way they lock onto mine—it punches the breath from my lungs.

Green. Wide. Luminous with something I want to believe is awe.

She's everything I'd dreamed of when I paid for Eden's services. The soft curve of her lips, the delicate line of her throat, the way she moves like she doesn't yet realize she belongs to me, just as *I* belong to *her*.

But beneath it, there's something else.

Fear.

It flickers in her gaze, just for a moment, a deer poised on the edge of flight. My mouth parts as a sharp worry slices through me.

Is she going to run?

The thought is unbearable. I take a half step forward, my muscles taut with the urge to reach for her, to reassure her before the moment fractures. Before she slips through my fingers.

The officiant tuts disapprovingly. Maybe because, for this marriage to be valid, she must come all the way to me. But I don't care. I extend my hand anyway.

She hesitates. I see it in the way her breath catches, the way her fingers tremble at her sides.

Of course she's afraid. She's never seen me before— never laid eyes on the man who is about to be her husband. This is all new, unknown. And the unknown is terrifying.

That's why she needs me.

This is when I step up. When I steady her, guide her, *claim* her proudly as my wife.

She only has to take my hand.

EIGHT

MORGAN

His hand hovers in the air as he patiently waits for me to take it. My gaze goes from his hand to his eyes, and I can feel the confidence coming off him, like he knows I'll take his hand.

Part of me wants to refuse, to turn away and go back to my grim reality where this man doesn't exist. Because at least then, I could live, knowing that I never deserved it anyway. But I don't. I'm *desperate* for this fever dream to be real.

And despite the fear shaking me to my core, I take his hand.

His fingers are warm, strong, and when they close around mine, there's a finality to it, like a lock clicking into place.

I can't tear my eyes away from our hands. His touch doesn't feel alien, like I thought it would. It doesn't feel like I'm holding onto a stranger. Instead, it feels strangely familiar, like we've known each other all our lives.

The officiant clears his throat, unimpressed, but I

barely hear him. My pulse is hammering in my ears as I force myself to finally look up—really look at the man standing before me.

He is breathtaking.

That should be my first red flag.

Men like this don't exist—not outside of books or movies or the unrealistic, airbrushed romances that show up in advertisements for places like Eden. And despite that fact, here he is. His navy suit fits like it was sewn to his body. His hair is dark, neatly styled, but not stiff. And his eyes—God, his eyes. They drink me in with an intensity that is both thrilling and terrifying.

I swallow hard, my lips parting before I can stop myself. "What's your name?"

His mouth lifts slightly into the softest smile, like the question amuses him, but his voice is smooth and steady when he answers.

"Henry Langford."

Henry.

Said like a man whose name has *weight*. The name rolls through me, settling in my chest, as if it should mean something. But it doesn't. He's a stranger. A stranger whose ring will be on my finger in less than five minutes.

His gaze softens. "And you?"

The words feel strange. Not just the question, but the way he asks it—like he already knows, but wants to hear it from my lips.

I hesitate, straighten my spine, and lift my chin. I say my name like it's got weight too, even if it really doesn't weigh much more than a blade of grass. "Morgan Sloane."

Henry smiles then. And it's beautiful.

For a moment, I feel the tension slip away.

It doesn't matter that this is absurd, that I am standing in a wedding hall with a man I have never met before, that my entire future is balancing on the edge of an application I made only a handful of days ago while I was desperate and heartbroken and lonely.

He is perfect.

And maybe, just maybe, this is real.

I barely notice the officiant shifting in front of us until his voice slices through the moment, sharp and dry. "Apologies, but we should carry on with this. There are other appointments."

I flinch at the sudden crack in the perfect day.

But Henry doesn't.

His head tilts slightly, and his expression—though still perfectly composed—hardens just enough that the officiant notices.

"I wasn't aware we were on a time limit," Henry says smoothly.

The officiant's lips thin. He glances between us, clearly debating whether to push back. He doesn't. Instead, he sighs and flips through the crisp white pages of the contract in his hands. "Fine. Let's proceed."

I don't know why, but my stomach tightens.

The way Henry stood up for me—subtly, but firmly—should be reassuring. And it is. But it's also... something else. Something that prickles along the back of my neck.

I push the feeling away.

The officiant drones on, a wide smile spreading across his face like nothing ever happened. I don't pay much attention to what he has to say. The words blur together, because all of my attention is on the man standing before me. It's strange, how the entire process feels hazy, like I'm watching it happen instead of living it.

So it's a shock when I hear my own voice, soft and breathless, saying, "I do."

Henry looks deep in my eyes, and in a low murmur, he says, "I do."

Before the officiant even asked him.

Henry takes my hand, and my breath stutters.

The band is smooth, cool against my skin, but it's the *diamond* that makes my heart stop. It's massive. A brilliant, impossible thing, catching the light and scattering rainbows across my fingers.

For a moment, I find myself struggling to breathe.

It's stunning.

It's unreal.

It's *mine*.

I stare at it, completely transfixed, hardly noticing the way Henry's thumb brushes over my knuckles, the way his lips quirk into a small, knowing smile.

"It looks beautiful on you," he murmurs.

Tears prick my eyes. I nod, unable to form words.

The officiant clears his throat gently, and I force myself to focus as I take Henry's ring—smaller, simpler, but just as significant. My hands tremble as I slide it into place, my fingers barely closing around his as I whisper, "Perfect fit."

Henry's eyes soften, something warm and unreadable flickering in them.

Then the fatal words come.

"You may now kiss the bride."

For a second, neither of us move.

And then, slowly, Henry reaches out, one hand cupping my face, his fingers brushing along my cheek with such reverence, such certainty, that I nearly shudder.

I should be nervous. I should be questioning everything. But when his lips meet mine, my mind empties.

Heat surges through me, melting away the last threads of hesitation.

He kisses me like he already owns me. Like I am something rare and precious that he has waited his entire life for.

And maybe that should be another red flag.

But right now, it feels like a promise, coming on silent angel wings.

When he pulls back, my lips are tingling, and my heart is hammering against my ribs, and I know—without a shadow of a doubt—that I made the right choice.

He is perfect.

And this is real.

Isn't it?

I lean into him slightly, letting the warmth of his body steady me. He presses his hand against the small of my back, guiding me away from the altar, away from the officiant who is already gathering his things, muttering something under his breath with that performative smile having evaporated.

I don't care.

All that matters is Henry.

My husband.

The man who was chosen for me.

I glance up at him, and know that whatever Eden wants to charge me, whatever price they demand, I would happily pay it.

Henry smiles down at me and before I can say anything, he leans down, lips brushing against my ear.

"Let's find our room."

The words send a shiver down my spine.

Not because I'm afraid, but because, for the first time in a long time, I'm *not*.

A laugh bubbles out of me, light and breathless, and before I even realize what I'm doing, I lurch forward, grabbing Henry's hand and pulling him with me. My dress catches at my ankles as I break into a sprint, my heartbeat wild, my mind spinning with something reckless and electric.

Henry's deep chuckle rumbles behind me, and then suddenly, his arms wrap around me. A gasp rips from my throat as my feet lift off the ground. He swings me up effortlessly with a gentle, but strong grip.

We fly past the hall, past Dexter's voice calling after us—

"Congratulations, Morgan, on your newfound Eden!"

I barely hear him. My laughter turns into a squeal as my bouquet tumbles from my hands, the flowers scattering across the path like an offering to the wind.

Henry doesn't slow. If anything, he runs faster, the ocean breeze whipping through my hair, the scent of salt and warm sand curling around us. We pass the lower-end rooms, the empty pool in the pristine courtyard, the silent staff who barely spare us a glance as they carry out their tasks, like this is an everyday occurrence in this strange, perfect world.

Still, he doesn't stop.

His breathing is even, his pace unbroken, like I weigh nothing at all.

And then, suddenly, we are at the top, where the suite waits.

My breath catches as I take it all in—the stretch of the ocean, endless and glittering beneath the setting sun. The soft glow of lanterns flickering along the terrace. The vast, sprawling room beyond the massive double doors, framed by arched windows and gauzy white curtains billowing in the wind.

It is dreamlike. Perfect.

But none of it—not the view, not the sky painted in hues of gold and lavender—compares to the man holding me.

Henry's gray eyes are locked on mine. Intense. Unreadable.

A slow, knowing smile curves my lips as he slows in front of the door, his grip adjusting slightly. But there's something... strange in his expression. A hesitation.

"What is it?" I ask, tilting my head.

He exhales, his fingers tightening against my back. "I'd like to carry you over the threshold," he says, his voice quieter now. More careful. "But I want to make sure you're comfortable. We... we don't have to go in just yet. We can get dinner, get to know each other first."

Something warm flickers inside me at the words. He's considerate. Thoughtful. Exactly the kind of man I had hoped for, but never dared to dream existed.

I know what Tiana would say. She would tell me to take him up on his offer, to take my time and get to know him before giving up something I couldn't take back. And yet, I don't want to wait. I don't want a slow, careful unraveling of whatever this is supposed to be.

I want *him*.

The thrill of it thrums in my veins, a hunger both unfamiliar and undeniable.

We have the rest of our lives to learn the little things about each other. The details, the quirks, the small, quiet intimacies that come with time.

But right now—

I want to claim him.

I want him to know—without hesitation, without a single doubt—that he is *mine*, for now and always.

A surge of confidence I haven't felt in ages passes through me, and I brush my fingertips along his jaw. A current of desire sparks under my skin, and the need to be closer to him, all of him, grows stronger with every beat of my pounding heart.

"Henry," I whisper, brushing my lips against his ear, letting my breath ghost over his skin. "Kick open the door."

Henry stiffens, just for a second. He looks genuinely shocked, like he fully expected me to take him up on his offer. Something about having caught him so off guard sends a thrill of pleasure through me.

Something shifts in his expression. The hesitation melts away, replaced by something darker. Something satisfied.

He moves.

One sharp motion—his leg jerking up, his foot slamming against the double doors. The force of it sends the doors bursting open, the hinges groaning in protest.

With a deep, low chuckle, Henry carries me over the threshold. Just the way a husband should.

The doors drift shut behind us with a quiet click.

But just before they do, a strange, overwhelming feeling grips me—something raw and unfamiliar.

Was that fear?

NINE

HENRY

It's early morning when I unwind myself from the covers
—and from my wife's tangling limbs. I stand over the bed,
watching her, taking her in. I wasn't sure what I expected
when I signed up for Eden's service, but it's all paid off.

Because last night was more than I ever dreamed of. I
can't remember the last time a woman left *me* breathless.

With a smirk, I brush a strand of hair from her face.
She stirs in her sleep, a slow, contented sigh leaving her
lips before she settles again.

"I'll be back," I murmur, just in case she's more awake
than she seems.

I pull on a pair of linen trousers and step outside. I
light a cigarette. The air is thick with salt and heat, the
distant crash of waves muffled by the resort's manicured
perfection. The sun hasn't risen yet, and the sky is still
that deep, endless dark—the kind that makes you wonder
if you'll ever see the light again.

I flick ash from the cigarette, watching it scatter into
the soft breeze. I take another slow drag, closing my eyes

as the rush of nicotine spreads through me, grounding me.

Cigarettes will be the death of me.

But we all have our vices. Some people shovel fried food into their stomachs. Others shoot up drugs. Some destroy everything around them with gambling.

I'm not one of those people. I'm a good man. I keep my nose clean, my wallet full, and my life stable. So what if I smoke now and then?

I shake my head, running a hand through my hair, and take another drag. The tension knotted deep in my gut starts to loosen. Hopefully, this will all work out. I'm not sure I can go back to the man I was before I was married.

Briefly, I wonder if Morgan knows just how pathetic and desperate I am.

I hope not.

She looks at me like I'm a man—like I'm something solid, something desirable. Masculine. It's been a long time since anyone's looked at me that way. Last thing I need is to ruin that illusion.

A speck appears on the distant horizon, just as the night sky begins to soften at the edges. I watch it, cigarette hovering at my lips. A bird, maybe. But the speck grows, moving too fast for a bird.

A plane.

A cold, crawling feeling settles in my gut as it approaches the resort's private strip.

I take another drag, longer this time, my eyes locked on the plane as it lands. The door opens. A silhouette emerges, too far to make out. Resort staff swarm the steps, gathering belongings, moving with well-practiced efficiency. The silhouette crosses the strip, heading toward what I know must be one of Eden's people.

I can't tell who they are. But something about the way they walk stops me cold.

I take another drag, inhaling deep, but it does nothing to settle the feeling creeping up my spine.

The silhouette moves with purpose, cutting across the tarmac. The way she carries herself—shoulders squared, strides long but unhurried—it's familiar.

I know that walk.

How did she find me here? Maybe the better question is *why* is she here?

The staff move around her, collecting luggage, speaking in low murmurs, but she doesn't pause. Doesn't glance at them. She has her eyes set on something.

Or someone.

A prickle travels over my skin, leaving goosebumps in its wake. I shift against the railing nervously, rubbing a hand over the stubble along my jaw.

Maybe Eden found her a match too.

But something about that thought doesn't sit right. Should it? I shake my head. Eden is a service. A system. I shouldn't care who she ends up with—not if that silhouette is really who I think it is.

But if she's here...

I shake my head, forcing a breath through my nose. Doesn't matter.

I have a wife now, sleeping peacefully in my bed. Whoever the silhouette is—whoever she used to be to me —she's the least of my worries.

Still, as I stub my cigarette out on the railing and head back inside, I can't shake the feeling creeping under my skin.

I hope I'm wrong.

God, I hope I'm wrong.

TEN
MORGAN

We had the option to have breakfast brought to our room, but I wanted to enjoy the resort while I could—at the pool. That was *after* I'd had a morning session with my new husband. I flush at the memory, my cheeks warming with the echo of it.

My gaze drifts to Henry, lounging in his chair with sunglasses perched on his nose, staring out at the horizon. His linen shirt is half-buttoned, exposing a glimpse of his chest, and a familiar heat stirs inside me. I exhale, forcing myself to calm down. Now I see why people glorify not just sex, but that deeper connection everyone craves—there's something intoxicating about finally *having* what you've spent years yearning for.

A man approaches with a tray of food, his smile bright and practiced. He sets it on the table, then pours two glasses of orange juice.

"If there's anything else you need, please let me know. I'm at your service."

"Thank you," I say. "This looks wonderful. We really appreciate it."

He blinks, surprise flickering in his eyes before he glances at Henry. Maybe guests here aren't known for their gratitude. I've seen the movies—rich people can be snobs, treating staff like they're invisible.

"It's my pleasure," the man says, giving a short bow before stepping away.

I grab a piece of pita bread and scoop a generous dollop of hummus onto it. I must be farther from home than I realized, given that everything on the table screams Mediterranean. If I'm honest, I was expecting something more... American. Maybe even touristy. I guess I'd hoped for pancakes at the very least.

But the second the hummus hits my tongue, I let out a small moan of pure satisfaction. Forget pancakes—this is *incredible*. I barely notice the rest of the food. I just keep going for the hummus, and Henry laughs.

"You like it, huh?"

I nod, swallowing before answering. "The Mediterranean food back home is nothing like this."

"Not good?"

"Worse." I wrinkle my nose. "It's terrible."

"So where are you from?"

I hesitate, feeling a little shy. "Des Moines. In Iowa. Our public transport's not great, and the Mediterranean food is even worse."

He smiles. "What about you?"

"Texas."

My brows lift. "You're from Texas?"

He shrugs. "I've been everywhere. My family moved

around a lot, but I figured Texas was a good place to settle."

"Why?" I try not to sound too skeptical, but I've heard my share of stories about Texas.

"Taxes, better roads, friendly folks. Lots of reasons."

I glance down, reminding myself this is my husband now. Chances are, *I'll* be moving there too—and soon. I push away the mild unease that creeps into my stomach, forcing myself to keep an open mind.

Henry leans back in his chair, sunglasses hiding his eyes, but I sense he's watching me carefully.

"If you end up not liking Texas, we can always find someplace new."

I blink. "You'd be willing to move?"

"For you? Of course. I want you to be happy."

Something about the way he says it—so easily, with such *certainty*—makes my stomach twist.

"But what about your work? Your business or whatever?"

He laughs, low and amused. "What makes you think I have a business?"

"Come on, take a look at yourself," I scoff. "You scream money. Not in a flashy way—no gaudy designer logos or anything like that—but in a quiet way. And that tells me you've got *serious* money."

He tilts his head, considering, the corner of his mouth lifting just enough to let me know I'm right. "Well, I'm a lucky man. And a free one. My work doesn't require my constant attention."

"What does that mean?"

He exhales, rolling his shoulders back like the conversation is almost boring him. "Most of my wealth comes from real estate and oil. The rest is tied up in businesses I have a vested interest in, sure, but that's why I sit on the board and hire a CEO to run them."

I stare at him. "You hired a CEO?"

He leans in slightly, his voice dropping, like he's letting me in on something intimate. "I'm a newlywed, Morgan. I have more important things to focus my time on than mundane work."

I wait for him to laugh. To smirk. To say he's joking.

But he doesn't. He just looks at me, perfectly serious.

He leans back, crosses his ankles, and pops a grape into his mouth like he doesn't have a care in the world. I shake my head, turning my focus back to my food.

It feels surreal. Like something ripped straight from a Hallmark movie.

I can practically see the blurb now:

Poor librarian, desperate for a fresh start, signs up for marriage at first sight—only to find herself paired with a man wealthier than she ever imagined.

All that's missing now is a little conflict.

But that's a movie. And somehow, this is real life. I exhale, forcing myself to relax. I should be grateful. I'm lucky, that's all.

As I take another bite, the atmosphere around us begins to shift. More couples begin filtering in for breakfast, settling at tables beneath the large white umbrellas lining the poolside. A few venture toward the water, their laughter low and indulgent. There's something strangely elegant about it all—no kids running wild, no screaming, no chaos. Just adults enjoying a morning in paradise.

I lean back, sipping my juice, letting myself soak in the luxury.

A waiter approaches, holding a small, folded card. With a courteous nod, he places it beside Henry's plate.

"A message, sir, from your Eden representative," he says smoothly. "As part of your package, Eden provides marriage counseling sessions with an on-site therapist. They suggested that you appear five minutes before the listed time."

"What?" I ask, reaching for the folded card. As I unfold it, I ask, "What do we need a therapist for?"

I'd hoped to see more information, but the card only listed a location on the resort and a time we were expected to appear. Worried, I glance up at Henry.

"I wouldn't overthink it, Morgan," Henry says. "It's part of the process."

"It is?" I don't remember reading anything about therapy, nor do I remember Dexter mentioning it. Maybe I hadn't been paying attention.

I bite my lip in concern but force myself to get over it. I'd always heard that early marriage counseling provided some really good benefits to the long term health of the marriage.

Maybe this wasn't a bad thing. In fact, maybe this was actually necessary, given that Henry and I still had so much to learn about each other.

"It's supposed to strengthen our bond as newlyweds," Henry says. "What time is it supposed to be?"

"Thirty minutes from now."

He nods, "We can finish breakfast, then go."

He looks to the waiter. "I trust that you'll escort us to our first session?"

"If that is what you wish, I would be happy to put myself at your service and pleasure."

"Perfect," Henry says, settling back into his chair and adjusting his sunglasses. "Come get us in twenty minutes when we've finished our breakfast."

"Of course, sir." The waiter dips his head and retreats.

"Therapy... Eden's more thorough than I thought," I say, attempting to keep my tone light.

He chuckles, "I suppose they want to make sure we stay happy, huh?"

I hum in agreement, but something about it nags at me. Not in a bad way—just in a *'this is odd, right?'* kind of way. Still, I push the thought aside. This is a luxury resort, and Eden was an ultra luxury, exclusive service. It makes sense that they'd go the extra mile to ensure their matches had the best chances of succeeding with their marriage.

With a relenting sigh, I take a few more bites of my food, my gaze wandering lazily over the other couples at the resort. Henry's closed his eyes, taking a moment to rest in the sun. I don't blame him. I must have worn him out last night, and I know he'd gotten up early to smoke.

Didn't love that, but hey, it was part of who he was. If a little smokey smell on him was the worst thing I had to deal with from time to time, then I was a lucky gal.

Then, from the corner of my eye, I see her.

A woman stands at the edge of the pool, smoothing a sheer cover-up over toned legs, dark hair cascading over one shoulder. Even from a distance, she's striking—the kind of beauty that makes you look twice.

I feel something, sharp and uncomfortable. Jealousy? Doubt? I don't know. All I know is that I wish she wasn't so beautiful.

I sneak a glance at Henry.

He doesn't seem to notice her. He's still lounging, still completely at ease.

But she notices him, and she's staring. Not a casual glance, not a passing look, but full-on *staring*.

My stomach twists.

I push the tray of food away, my appetite having suddenly soured. I try to take another sip of juice and shake the feeling. Maybe I'm overthinking it. Maybe I'm being ridiculous. After all, Henry was an extremely attractive man, and as his wife, I suppose that this wasn't the first time I was going to find another woman staring at my man.

This was normal.

But still.

I wish she'd look somewhere else.

ELEVEN

MORGAN

The therapy office is sleek, modern, and nothing like the sterile, overly bright spaces I always associated with counseling. The walls are a soothing shade of taupe, and the large floor-to-ceiling windows overlook a garden filled with exotic plants, a small fountain bubbling in the center. It's weird to think, but it's almost too perfect. It feels like I'm sitting on a movie set or something.

But to be fair, this entire place was that way. I suppose those movie sets were made to resemble *something*. And this? This would be great inspiration to capture an ideal that most people could only ever dream existed.

Henry and I sit side by side in comfortable chairs, the kind that swallows you just enough to make you feel at ease, but not enough to make you forget where you are. Across from us, in a single sleek armchair, sits our therapist.

She smiles warmly, her dark hair smoothed into a

pristine bun, a simple pearl necklace resting at the base of her throat.

"Welcome, welcome, Mr. and Mrs. Langford," she says, folding her hands over the tablet on her lap.

It takes me a second to remember that's *me*. I'm Mrs. Langford now. Not Ms. Sloane.

"I'm Dr. Elise Warren, your Eden counselor, and I'll be guiding you both through your first session."

Her voice is soft, measured, like someone who has perfected the art of making people feel safe in her presence. I already know her type—calm, collected, with that reassuring half-smile that makes you feel like no matter what you say, she's already heard worse.

"I know therapy can feel daunting for some," she continues, "but think of this as a continued wellness check for your marriage. Here at Eden, we believe that a strong foundation leads to lifelong success. And as part of our exclusive service, these sessions will ensure that you two start on the right path together."

I nod, shifting slightly. "Makes sense."

It'd be great if I had my phone so I could look her up, check her reviews and her credentials. Unfortunately, I don't. So I'm forced to trust that she knows what she's on about. But if Eden picked her to ensure the success of their matches, then I'm sure she *does*.

"Good," she says, tapping something onto her tablet before looking back up at us. "Now, let's begin. How was your first night together?"

I blink. "Our... first night?"

Beside me, Henry chuckles, reaching over to rest his

hand on my thigh. "There's only one word for it. Spectacular."

I feel my cheeks warm. "It was great."

Dr. Warren tilts her head at my response, her eyes staring deep into my soul. "Honesty is going to be a pillar of your success here. Are you sure it was great, Morgan?"

Out of the corner of eye, I see Henry's smile falter, and a little doubt creeps into his expression. I bristle as I focus my attention back on Dr. Warren.

"I'm positive. It was like Henry said. Spectacular."

Henry's smile returns, and I breathe a sigh of relief.

"That's wonderful to hear. Would you say you *felt* the spark? That instant connection you both craved?"

I glance at Henry as he answers. "Absolutely. I knew the moment I saw her."

His words land smoothly, perfectly, without a hint of hesitation. I smile, pushing away a tiny flutter of self-consciousness. "Yeah. I think we really clicked."

Dr. Warren hums, tapping again. "Good, good. And intimacy-wise? Did it feel natural? Comfortable?"

I shift in my seat. I'm not sure why she's digging so much into this. "I mean... yeah. Of course."

Henry's grip on my thigh tightens slightly, and I look into his grey eyes, letting them ground me.

Still looking at me, he says, "It was perfect. *She's* perfect."

Dr. Warren's eyes flick to me, studying me for a second too long before nodding. "That's exactly what we want to hear."

The session continues in much the same way—question after question, all slightly invasive but framed as casual, harmless inquiries. Are we happy so far? Have we had a chance to get to know each other? Do we feel like we complement each other? Are there any early concerns?

Henry answers every question smoothly, confidently. He doesn't stumble, doesn't hesitate. He says all the right things.

For some reason, I can't shake the feeling that this is... rehearsed. But maybe that's the way therapy is. After all, Dr. Warren must sit in these sessions day after day, going over the same questions each time.

Then Dr. Warren sets her tablet aside, smiling at me. "Morgan, would you mind stepping out for a moment?"

I blink. "What?"

"It's standard practice," she assures me. "We conduct a brief personal session with each spouse to check in individually. Nothing to worry about."

I glance at Henry, but he seems completely at ease, already leaning back into the couch.

"Oh," I say, standing slowly. "Okay. Sure."

Dr. Warren gestures toward the door. "The lounge just outside has refreshments. Feel free to help yourself. This won't take long."

I hesitate, but nod, slipping out of the office and into the hallway.

The door clicks shut behind me, and that's when I notice the couple approaching.

The man isn't what you'd call conventionally handsome—long hair, a rounded face framed by a thick mustache, built like a bear. But there's kindness in his eyes, which is more than I can say for the woman beside him, her hand resting lightly in the crook of his arm.

It's *her*.

The woman from the pool. The one who had stared at Henry without a shred of shame.

Now, she's staring at me.

Her gaze is unwavering, cool, detached—as if she's looking at something *less* than her, something unworthy of a reaction. As much as I hate it, the only thought that appears in my mind as a response is... she smells *good*. I don't really know perfumes—I don't wear any myself—but whatever she's wearing, it has this nice twist of rose and... musk?

The man clears his throat, offering a smile. "Hey there, sorry to bother you, but this is where the counselor is, right?"

I don't look away from her when I answer. "Yeah. You're in the right place."

"Great," he says with a nervous laugh. A moment of awkward silence lingers before he shifts, then offers his hand. "I'm Brody. This is—"

"Genevieve," she finishes, her voice smooth, effortless. She doesn't extend her hand.

She just keeps watching me.

"That's right, but she goes by—" Brody starts.

"Just Genevieve," she cuts him off, offering me a thin, practiced smile.

His own smile falters for half a second before he clears his throat, recovering quickly.

"Nice to meet you," I say, keeping my voice even. "I'm Morgan. Did you two meet through Eden too?"

"We did." Brody's smile returns, and he glances down at Genevieve, looking at her like she's the best thing that's ever happened to him. "Couldn't believe my luck, you know? Not a whole lot of women like her where I'm from. Shoot, not a whole lot of women like her *anywhere*."

Genevieve's lips press into a thin line. She tilts her head, looking up at him. "You're too kind."

Poor Brody.

He has no idea she's not into him. Not even a little.

Then again, who am I to judge? Maybe she's just going through an adjustment period. They're still here, still married, and if Eden matched them, then they must know something I don't. Maybe this is exactly why the marriage counseling sessions exist—to help couples struggling to settle into their new reality.

Genevieve turns back to me, slipping her hand from Brody's arm and folding both in front of her. "Where's your husband?"

"He's inside," I say, trying to keep my tone neutral. "They're just wrapping up."

Her eyebrow lifts slightly. "You're not in there with him?"

"No," I answer, shifting on my feet. I hate that she's making me feel on edge. "Individual sessions are part of it, I guess."

"Hmm."

My blood heats. I really do not like her.

I tilt my head. "Didn't I see you earlier?"

She doesn't blink. "Maybe."

We hold each other's stare for a beat too long.

There's something unsettling about the way she looks at me—like she's waiting for something. A reaction, maybe. Some sign that I'm intimidated by her.

I'm not normally one for confrontation, but this time, I force myself to stand my ground. Henry was *mine*.

I shift my weight, tilting my head just slightly. Not quite a challenge, but not backing down either. If she's expecting me to flinch, she'll be waiting a long time.

Genevieve's lips twitch, but she doesn't smile.

Before either of us can say anything else, the office door clicks open behind me, and Henry steps out the door, running a hand through his hair, still lost in thought. His gaze lifts, quickly finding mine, and his lips curve into a gentle smile. Warmth floods through me, dissolving some of the tension.

"There you are," he says, taking a step closer. Before he can say another word, I close the distance between us, sliding my hand to the back of his neck, pulling him into a deep, possessive kiss. Surprise stiffens his posture for just a second before his arms slide around my waist, his lips softening under mine as he leans into the embrace.

When I pull away, I brush my fingers over Henry's jaw, letting my lips linger close to his.

"Everything go okay?" I ask, keeping my voice just soft enough for only him to hear.

His grip on me tightens before he exhales a short breath, recovering.

"Yeah," he murmurs with a soft smile.

Then I feel him tense suddenly, his grip tightening. Pulling back slightly, I glance up to see his gaze locked onto Genevieve and Brody, still watching us. A faint flush rises to Henry's cheeks, his expression shifting to something unreadable. Unease slithers into my stomach.

Genevieve's eyes narrow slightly, flicking from Henry to me. I sense the calculation beneath her calm exterior. I meet her gaze evenly, lifting my chin just a fraction.

Brody clears his throat and takes a step forward, extending his hand toward Henry. "Hey man, nice to meet you. I'm Brody. And this is Genevieve."

Henry blinks, like he's just snapping out of something. He releases me and shakes Brody's hand, his usual smile slipping into place.

"Henry Langford," he says.

He turns to Genevieve, but she doesn't extend her hand. She simply watches. There's a strange sort of tension in the air that I don't like.

I thread my fingers with Henry's and lean in, "Ready to go?"

Henry turns his attention back to me, and his shoulders relax. "Yeah. Let's head out."

Genevieve's eyes linger on us a moment longer before she offers a smooth, insincere smile. Brody remains oblivious, still grinning like a man who believes he's won the lottery.

"Nice meeting you both," I say, my voice steady despite the thudding of my heart.

"Likewise," Genevieve responds, her voice a soft murmur. But her eyes betray something else entirely.

"Good luck with the counseling," I say to Brody, before Henry leads me away.

He's got a firm grip on my hand, and a tight silence hangs between us. I'm not sure why he's so tense. Maybe he's just not comfortable with public displays of affection. I'd met men like that before. It always puzzled me, but I had to acknowledge that everyone was different.

Behind us, Genevieve's eyes burn into my back, but I don't look over my shoulder. I know I've made my point clear enough.

Henry belongs to me.

TWELVE
MORGAN

We're lying tangled in bed, my fingertips tracing idle patterns along Henry's chest, the dim light casting reflections off my diamond ring. He's warm, his skin pressed gently to mine, and I allow myself to sink into the sensation, to savor something I've longed for longer than I care to admit.

I should be lost in this moment—wrapped up entirely in my new husband—but instead, my mind drifts stubbornly back to her. Genevieve. Even her name is ostentatious. She had money written all over her, from her perfect posture to that icy confidence in her eyes.

"Hey," I murmur softly, nudging Henry with my fingertips. "Can I ask you something?"

"Mmm." His voice is sleepy, satisfied. "Of course."

I tilt my chin up to look at him, watching the relaxed lines of his face. "What did you think of that couple earlier? Brody and... Genevieve?"

The peaceful look slips from Henry's face. He

doesn't exactly tense, but his posture changes subtly beneath me—just enough to let me know this isn't a topic he wants to discuss. My stomach tightens.

"They seemed nice enough," he says carefully.

I scoff lightly, propping myself on my elbow to study his face better. "You really thought they seemed nice?"

He shrugs, brushing a strand of hair from my eyes. "I didn't notice anything unusual. Why—did you?"

I consider lying, shrugging it off, pretending Genevieve's cold gaze hadn't bothered me. But instead, I press my lips together and give a half-hearted shrug of my own. "I don't know. She seemed a little... intense. Kind of cold, you know?"

He studies me for a beat too long. "Did she say something to upset you?"

"No, not exactly." I shake my head, embarrassment flushing my cheeks. "But I did see her at breakfast, full-on staring at you."

He holds his breath for a moment, then lets it out in an exasperated sigh. "Can you really blame her?"

I blink at him, frowning slightly. "What's that supposed to mean?"

He wiggles his eyebrows playfully. "Have you seen me? I've got abs, my love."

I roll my eyes, smacking his arm lightly, but a reluctant smile creeps across my lips. "You're ridiculous."

"And you love it." He grins, effortlessly disarming me. He reaches forward, brushing a loose strand of hair behind my ear, fingertips lingering on my skin. "Listen. We don't have to worry about other couples. We're here for us. Remember that."

I nod slowly, letting his words settle my racing thoughts. He's right—this is about us, not some random woman whose opinion shouldn't matter at all.

Yet even as I nestle back against him, I can't entirely shake the unease. Something about Genevieve just gets under my skin, and I don't like it.

"She was with that guy, Brody, right?" Henry says after a moment, voice casual.

"Yeah. Brody." I pause, smiling a little. "I actually liked Brody."

He shifts suddenly, rolling himself on top of me. He braces himself on his arms, looking down into my eyes, a teasing glint in his. "Oh? You liked him, huh?"

I laugh, wrinkling my nose. "Yeah, I did. I liked him a lot."

His eyes narrow playfully, and then his lips find mine. His kiss is firm, deep, almost possessive, stealing the breath from my lungs in an attempt to chase away all the doubts.

When he finally pulls back, I'm breathless beneath him.

"What was that for?" I ask.

"Just reminding you who your husband is," he murmurs, smirking against my lips. "Wouldn't want Brody getting any ideas."

I laugh again, pulling him down for another kiss. "You're ridiculous."

"And you like it."

I do. I really do.

But even as Henry kisses me again, slow and deep

and lingering, I can't help but think about Genevieve's cold stare.

And for some reason, it still bothers me.

THIRTEEN
HENRY

It's only when Morgan finally falls asleep that the uneasy feeling returns.

I stare up at the ceiling, my fingers gently stroking through her hair as her breathing evens out, her soft warmth grounding me in reality.

Throughout dinner, I'd managed to forget all about Genevieve's presence, focusing instead on the woman beside me—my beautiful, charming, unexpectedly perfect wife.

Everything about Morgan draws me in deeper: the idea of her cozy little apartment, the softness in her voice when she talks about the books she loves, and even the simple fact that she's a librarian.

She was different from every other woman I'd met before, and I was falling hard for her. She was everything I hoped Eden would find for me, and *so* much more.

I could tell she felt the same. She wanted to know everything about me. What my parents were like, if I had any pets, if I liked to read, what I did for fun. We even spoke about my twin sister, who I'd lost a long time ago.

Somehow, the conversation had flowed easily between us throughout the served courses of dinner, with no awkward pauses or uncertain silences. It moved effortlessly, back and forth, like waves against the shore—just as things should be.

But now, in the silence and the dark, I can't push *her* from my thoughts.

Those unfeeling eyes. That barely-there lift at the corner of her mouth—a subtle mockery that only I seemed to notice. She was hiding something. She knew something.

It was clear now how she was here. Supposedly she'd found love in that man, Brody. I'm not naive enough to believe it, though. Don't get me wrong, he seemed decent, earnest even, but Genevieve wasn't someone who'd settle for *earnestness*.

The remaining question still lingers in my mind.

Why was she here?

A heavy sigh escapes me, and I run a frustrated hand over my face. I can't dislodge the dread pooling deep in my stomach, whispering to me that things are about to unravel, quickly and violently.

My gaze shifts down to Morgan, sleeping peacefully, her dark hair cascading over the pillow, her lips slightly parted in gentle breaths. The thought of losing her, after finally finding someone who makes me feel *alive* again, sets my teeth on edge.

Carefully, I ease myself away from her and slip outside, smacking the cigarette pack against my palm before pulling one free. With an exasperated sigh, I light up and lean against the railing.

The stars are out in full force, the sky stretched wide and endless. A cool breeze whispers across my skin, raising goosebumps in its wake. I take a slow drag, letting the nicotine seep into my lungs, feeling the tension in my shoulders loosen just a little.

Smoke curls from my lips, rising toward the heavens.

Whatever cruel plans Genevieve has in store—whatever game she's playing—I won't let her near Morgan. Not this time.

Then it hits me. A creeping sensation, prickling along my spine.

Someone's watching.

I snap my head around, the ash scattering from my cigarette. My gaze sweeps the darkness, scanning for movement, for a shadow, for anything. But there's nothing. No one.

Maybe Morgan got up, peered at me through the door. Who knows.

But I don't think that's it.

Maybe it's an animal—a raccoon, a fox. Do they even have those out here?

Somehow, I doubt it.

I swallow hard, take another drag, then grind the cigarette against the railing. No point in smoking if I can't even enjoy it.

Slipping back inside, I climb into bed and brush a strand of hair from Morgan's face, careful not to wake her. She exhales softly, leaning into my touch, and warmth spreads through my chest, chasing away the chill. Slowly, the knot of unease loosens.

I draw her closer, whispering gently against her ear.

"You're mine."

And she is. Genevieve can't change that, no matter what she does.

FOURTEEN
MORGAN

I can't remember the last time I spent this long away from my phone—away from technology entirely. No notifications buzzing, no social media updates flooding my screen, no endless cycle of tragic news or mind-numbing articles designed to keep me scrolling forever. Just silence. Just stillness.

It's strange, this sudden freedom.

Time itself seems to stretch, the days unfolding at a slower, more deliberate pace. Without a phone to tether me to the digital world, I feel untangled, as if I've stepped outside of time entirely. The world around me feels bigger, fuller—like I'm finally noticing things that have always been there, waiting to be seen. The endless expanse of sky, the rhythmic pulse of the waves, the way the sand shifts and shimmers beneath the afternoon sun.

And, oddly, I don't miss it.

I don't miss the frantic scrolling, the curated perfection of other people's lives, or the constant demand for my attention. If anything, I want more of this—this quiet, this simplicity. Maybe when Henry and I return to the States and move into the house, we'll make it a rule. No screens for a weekend every month. Just us, just the real world, just the life we're building together. We'll immerse ourselves in the moment, in each other, in the kind of love that doesn't need validation from likes or comments.

A deep, satisfied breath escapes me as I float on my back in the rolling waves, letting the water cradle me. I've never been a strong swimmer, but here, the ocean is different. It's gentle, the waves more of a rhythmic lull than an overwhelming force. The warmth of the sun sinks into my skin, and the weight of the world—or at least the one I used to be trapped in—fades away.

A slow grin tugs at my lips.

Henry.

I still can't believe him.

Last night at dinner, I searched for a flaw, some tiny crack in his perfect exterior. Maybe he hated dogs. Maybe he had a strained relationship with his parents. Maybe—something. Anything. But instead, every word, every gesture, only reinforced what I already felt deep in my bones.

He is perfect.

And not in the way people throw the word around— no, Henry is perfect down to the marrow. Down to the way he listens, really listens, when I speak. Down to the way he looks at me, like I am something rare, something precious. Down to the way he makes me feel—like I'm the only woman in the world.

It makes what I felt for James seem laughable.

James was a boy, and Henry? Henry is the man I've spent my life searching for.

I sit up in the water, shake my hair back, the strands clinging to my skin as I let my gaze drift toward the beach in search of my husband. The sand is crowded with couples lounging under umbrellas, stretched out on chairs, sipping drinks, and basking in the golden warmth of the afternoon.

Some are wrapped in each other's arms, lost in whispers and laughter. Others are a little too close for what's probably considered appropriate in public, but the sight only makes my smile widen. There's something refreshing about it—this unrestrained affection, this willingness to revel in the moment.

I scan the shore, my eyes landing on a familiar figure.

Brody.

He sits alone in the sand, feet buried beneath it, staring absently at the water. When he notices me looking, he lifts a hand in an easy wave. I force a polite smile, nodding in return before shifting my attention elsewhere.

I'm not looking for him.

I'm looking for her.

Genevieve.

The name itself stirs something sharp and uneasy inside me. My muscles tense before I can stop them, the peaceful weightlessness I felt only moments ago already starting to slip away. She's out here somewhere. I can feel it.

My eyes sweep across the beach until they land on her.

Standing next to my husband.

She's wearing a bikini that somehow manages to be both scandalous and sophisticated, hugging every inch of her impossibly lithe frame. There isn't a single flaw on her—not a single bit of cellulite, not a single ounce of softness, nothing. Even the way her hair cascades down her back is like something out of a shampoo commercial, catching the sunlight in a way that makes it gleam.

I thought she was beautiful the first time I saw her.

But now?

Now, she makes runway models look ordinary. And worse—she makes me feel like I'm an ugly cow.

Jealousy slams into me, hot and ugly, burning in my chest like acid. I don't move, frozen at the sight of them together.

But then I look at Henry.

His posture is rigid, his shoulders stiff, his jaw locked so tightly I can see the muscle jumping from here. He won't even look at her.

The jealousy dissolves, replaced with a sharp, exhilarating thrill. He doesn't want her near him. He's uncomfortable—tense. That's a good sign. That's a great sign.

I make a mental note to reward him later.

Then she laughs. And as if that weren't enough, she presses her hand against Henry's bare chest.

Oh, *hell no.*

I don't even think—I just move.

Channeling my inner Michael Phelps, I swim hard, cutting through the water with single-minded purpose, though I probably resemble a splashing seal more than anything else.

The second my feet hit the sand, I'm up and moving,

stalking toward them. I'm all too aware of how different we look—her, flawless and toned, me, dripping wet, hair plastered to my skin, with a pouch for a stomach.

I grab a spare beach towel off a nearby stack and wrap it around myself, hating that I feel the need to.

The closer I get, the clearer their conversation becomes.

"Don't be so shocked, Henry," she says, her voice a breathy, teasing lilt.

Henry.

She says his name like she knows him. The familiarity of it grates against me.

She flicks her hair back over her shoulder, throws a smug little glance toward Brody—a sneer, really—before turning back to Henry with a perfectly curated smile.

"Of course I found someone. Brody's a wonderful man."

Henry shakes his head, his hands curling into fists at his sides.

She sees me approaching. I know because she shifts ever so slightly—just enough to block me from Henry, just enough to make me pick up my pace.

"So, how is Charlie these days?" she asks, voice as smooth as glass.

Charlie?

I don't hesitate. I step forward, right into Henry's space, pressing my body against his before tilting my head up to look at him.

He glances down at me, and for the briefest second, something flickers across his face. Relief, I think. Like he's just been handed a lifeline. Like I've saved him from drowning in whatever toxic game Genevieve is playing.

Still, I latch onto the name, my gaze snapping back to her.

"Charlie?" I ask, my tone sharper than I mean it to be.

It sounded like a pet name, with the way she said it. But I knew it couldn't be. His cat's name was Skylar, if I remembered right from dinner last night. So who was Charlie?

Genevieve's lips curl at the edges, eyes glinting.

"Oh," she murmurs, tilting her head. "She doesn't know?"

I bristle, every muscle in my body tightening, but I refuse to take the bait.

She lets the silence stretch, savoring it, dragging it out before delivering the punchline with a lazy smirk.

"Charlie's the name of his private chef."

His chef?

He never mentioned having a chef in the house.

I glance up at Henry. "I didn't know about Charlie."

He grimaces. A shadow flickers across his face, but before he can say anything, Genevieve steps in again, ever so helpful.

"Oh... well, Henry's closer to Charlie than just about anybody. Charlie was his parents' chef, practically raised him."

"Is that true?" My voice comes out sharper than intended. I can't help it. "How come you didn't mention Charlie last night at dinner, if he was so important?"

Henry exhales slowly, like he's measuring his words.

But before he can respond, Genevieve laughs, tossing her long hair over her shoulder.

"*He?* Charlie is a woman, Megan."

My spine stiffens.

"My name is *Morgan*," I snap.

She waves a hand, dismissive, like I'm beneath her notice.

"So, Charlie?" I press, turning back to Henry.

His hesitation stretches a beat too long. Then, finally, he says, "You know my parents worked a lot when I was younger. They hired Charlie as my nanny at first. But soon, they needed a chef, too. She sort of became both."

"Sort of?" Genevieve echoes with a chuckle. "Charlie is a wonderful cook. She—"

"Whatever," I say, cutting her off. Her laugh dries up, and she turns to me, eyes flashing. For a split second, the mask slips, and I see it. The pure, unfiltered hatred beneath.

Then, just as quickly, it's gone.

"Didn't realize the two of you were so close," I murmur.

Henry shakes his head. "We're not."

Genevieve lifts a brow, as if she might disagree.

"Eve—" Henry pauses, his teeth clenching. A flicker of frustration crosses his face, like he just stepped into a trap. He exhales. "Genevieve and I used to know each other growing up. But... life happened, and we grew apart."

I stare at him. *Eve.* He'd called her *Eve*, not *Genevieve*.

Life happened? And they grew apart?

I don't buy that. Not entirely. There's more to the story, I can feel it, and from the way he's looking at her now—a simmering, controlled anger—I'd bet my life on it. Henry doesn't like her. In fact, I get the sense he *hates* her. Like she's not supposed to be here. Like her presence is a violation of some rule.

"And now she's here," I say slowly, watching his reaction.

His mouth tightens. "Yeah."

I wait for an explanation. It doesn't come.

The heavy silence stretches.

A voice cuts through the tension.

"Hey, guys!"

Brody.

He comes jogging up to us, sand kicking up in his wake, his broad smile as bright as the afternoon sun. We all turn to him.

He's slightly out of breath as he slings an arm over Genevieve's shoulder. The moment his fingers touch her, she tilts her head toward him, her mouth curling at the corner in something that looks like affection—but isn't. Not quite.

It's subtle. Fleeting. But I catch it.

The expression is gone in an instant, wiped clean, replaced with something softer, sweeter. She looks up at Brody, her eyes sparkling with love.

He doesn't notice.

I do.

"What's happening over here?" he asks, looking at each of us in turn, his usual affable charm on full display.

Henry steps back, like he wants to disengage.

Genevieve smirks up at Brody, fingers idly tracing patterns along his arm.

"Nothing," she hums. "Just catching up."

"Catching up," I echo, my gaze sliding back to Henry. His shoulders are rigid, his expression unreadable.

But I know what I saw. And I know what I felt. Something isn't right. Genevieve isn't just *here*.

She's here for a reason.

"Ah, okay, okay, I see," Brody says, grinning. "Would love to be in the water, but well, can't swim. Crazy nice day though, isn't it? "

"Brody, let's go back to bed," she states, her gaze locked onto Henry before she turns, sauntering away with slow, deliberate sways of her hips. It's a performance, and we all fall for it, watching.

Brody tilts his head, blinking in surprise. He rubs his jaw, then chuckles, flashing us a wide, lazy grin.

"Well, when your woman calls... I'll see you guys later."

He jogs after her, and the moment he's gone, I hear the sharp exhale of breath beside me. Henry is still staring after them, his eyes filled with hatred. He drapes his arm over my shoulder. But for the first time, I don't feel warmth in his embrace.

I feel the heat of my own frustration, curling tight in my stomach like a slow burn.

I step out from under his arm, crossing mine over my chest. "Why didn't you say you knew her?"

Henry looks at me, almost astonished, like he can't believe I pulled away. His mouth hardens. He digs into his pocket, pulls out his pack of cigarettes, then whips one free and lights it with practiced ease.

"Don't tell me you're mad."

"Mad?" I let out a hollow laugh. "You lied to me."

"No, I didn't."

"You acted like you didn't know her."

"And I don't. Not really, anyway. I meant what I said. Life happened. We grew apart."

I shake my head. "So why does she know the name of your chef, Henry? And why does she act so familiar with you?"

His eyes darken. "I don't know, okay?"

The words snap out of him, sharp and defensive.

A few couples on the beach glance over, exchanging worried looks. Maybe they're wondering if we might be them. Maybe they should be, because if there's a crack in the perfection of Henry, then they're all in danger.

I don't say anything. I just stand there, breathing hard, waiting.

Henry takes a long drag, runs a hand through his hair, then exhales a slow stream of smoke. His mood shifts in an instant. He flicks the cigarette away, even though it's barely burned, then steps forward, arms wrapping around me.

"Look, what'd I say?" His voice is softer now, coaxing.

I don't answer, but I don't pull away either.

"I said we're here for us. Not anybody else. Right? Forget about her. She's nothing."

His fingers find my chin, tilting my face up until I'm forced to look into those stupid, beautiful eyes.

"You're the only one in my world right now. Okay?"

I nod. I even smile.

But something doesn't sit right. The way Genevieve looked at him. The way he looked at her.

She's nothing? Then why does she feel like something more?

The breeze coming off the ocean feels colder now, despite the sun beating down. I lean into Henry's touch, but my mind is elsewhere. I could let it go. I *should* let it go. Genevieve is just some woman from his past, and I'm his wife. The life we're building together is real. Solid.

But then I remember the flicker in Henry's eyes when he said her name. *Eve.* A slip of the tongue, maybe. Or maybe something more.

I glance back toward the beach, expecting to see Genevieve and Brody disappearing into the distance, but Genevieve isn't looking at Brody.

She's looking at me.

And she's smiling.

A slow, knowing smile. Like she's waiting for something.

A chill runs down my spine.

I could push. I could ask Henry more questions, demand more answers. Or I could let it go, bury the doubt, and pretend this day is as perfect as it's supposed to be.

I swallow hard and lace my fingers through his.

It'd be smarter to pretend. But I knew that the need to know wasn't going to go away. Not until I knew what *Eve's* connection to Henry was.

FIFTEEN

MORGAN

My mind is still stuck on Genevieve during dinner, leaving a strange tension hanging between Henry and me. Neither of us talks much. He's not looking my way, and I'm carefully avoiding his gaze, as if eye contact might cause more problems between us.

Instead, my eyes wander through the crowd, scanning the faces in search of answers. Who exactly is this *Eve* to my husband?

Then I see him—standing near the edge of the restaurant, deep in conversation with a staff member. I recognize him instantly by the tailored precision of his suit.

Dexter.

A rush of urgency grips me. I wipe my mouth, place my napkin gently on the table, and offer Henry a reassuring smile as I stand.

"I'll be right back," I say casually.

He looks at me, eyebrows drawn together, puzzled, but doesn't press for details. In fact, he seems almost relieved, like he's grateful for a moment alone to sort through whatever is troubling him. Maybe that's exactly what he needs—the tension from earlier is still palpable, and perhaps space will ease it.

But space won't help me. I need answers, and I need them now.

I move swiftly through the restaurant, threading carefully through tables and patrons, my heart rate quickening as Dexter starts to turn toward the exit. I raise a hand, waving urgently, desperate to catch his attention before he disappears.

"Excuse me. Sorry," I mutter, bumping past a woman coming from the restroom. I push out the door and see Dexter a short distance away. "Dexter!"

He pauses and looks back over his shoulder, one eyebrow raised.

I breathe a sigh of relief as I wave and catch up to him. "Hey, I haven't seen you in a while."

"I do my best to keep out of the way once matches are made. Especially when they seem to be going so well," he says with a wink. "But is there something I can help you with?"

"Actually, yes, there is." I bite my lip, carefully choosing how to phrase my question.

Dexter waits patiently, his eyes calm and attentive.

"I thought nobody would know each other here, but there's this woman—Genevieve?" I watch his face closely for any flicker of recognition, but his expression remains carefully neutral. "Anyway, it seems she knows Henry somehow."

A faint crease appears between his brows. It's subtle, but I notice it.

"It's uncommon for matched couples to know each other prior to Eden," he says thoughtfully, "but the world is small, especially among the elite. It's certainly possible they're familiar with each other."

"Right, sure," I say, shifting uncomfortably. "But were they ever together?"

Dexter pauses, studying me with mild amusement, and then a slow smile spreads across his face. "Mrs. Langford, are you jealous?"

I flush, shifting awkwardly from one foot to the other. "No, no, I'm not jealous. I'm just—well, I'm frustrated. I don't like not knowing their history."

"History?" Dexter's tone is reassuring, gentle even. "I assure you, there's no reason to worry. But perhaps you should raise these concerns during your marriage counseling sessions. Dr. Warren can guide you through these emotions and help you build stronger trust in your relationship."

I deflate slightly, disappointment sinking in my stomach. Maybe he's right. It is a small world, after all. Eden services only a small portion of the population, and it makes sense that some paths would inevitably cross.

But still, as Dexter offers another confident smile, I can't help feeling like he's dismissing a concern that's more serious than he wants to admit.

"Okay, maybe I will. Thanks, Dexter," I sigh.

"Is there anything else?" he asks.

I shake my head and offer him a farewell wave, turning away with a forced smile. My heart still flutters in uneasy beats as a small voice in the back of my mind warns me to not let this go. But I push it aside and head back into the restaurant.

There won't be any answers out here.

Henry glances up when I reach our table, worry etched into his face. He sets down his fork, leaning forward slightly as I sit.

"Everything okay?" he asks quietly, eyes scanning my face.

My throat feels tight, but I manage a nod. "Yeah," I say, mustering a small smile. "I'm fine. Just—tired, I guess. I think I might head back early and run a bath."

"Of course," he says gently, his expression softening. "Are you sure you're all right, though?"

I don't want to lie, but I can't bring myself be honest either. Not yet.

"I promise," I reply, reaching across the table to squeeze his hand. "You stay and finish dinner. I'll see you back at the suite."

He studies me for a moment longer, then sighs and gives me a little nod. "Okay, I'll settle the bill and join you soon."

"Take your time," I say, rising from my chair and slipping through the dining room. Part of me still wants to stay and press Henry for answers, but forcing the topic now will only escalate my anxiety. And the last thing I need is more eyes on us in a crowded restaurant.

Outside, a warm breeze brushes across my skin, bringing the scent of the ocean. I walk briskly across the resort grounds, my sandals clicking against the stone path. The moon shines overhead, pale and serene.

Despite the questions swirling around in my mind

about Genevieve, maybe Dexter's right. Maybe this is all just a coincidence, and nothing is as big as it seems. It would be incredibly uncharacteristic of Eden to make a mistake like this.

By the time I reach our suite, I've worked myself into a half-hearted acceptance: This is something I can't solve in one frantic night. I think Dexter had a point—this might be best addressed in counseling, where we could air our baggage, piece by piece, until all the worry unraveled.

Inside, the soft glow of recessed lighting soothes me somewhat. I drop my evening clutch onto the entry table and head straight for the bathroom. The tub is massive, outfitted with chrome fixtures and sprinkled with flower petals by the staff—a typical Eden flourish that usually makes me smile. But tonight, I barely notice them.

I turn on the taps, letting hot water spill into the porcelain. My reflection in the mirror catches my eye: a subtle frown wrinkles my forehead, making me look older, wearier. With a deep breath, I slip out of my dress and lower myself into the steaming bath, water lapping around my tense muscles.

I draw a deep breath of the steam swirling through the air, and feel myself relax. Everything would be fine. Everything would work itself out. After all, we'd both come here to build a future together, not to bury secrets.

I sink lower, allowing myself to drift off, until the faint click of the suite door pulls me back to full awareness.

"Hey," Henry's voice calls softly through the half-open bathroom door. "You doing okay?"

I sit up, water sloshing around me.

"Yeah," I answer, a little breathless.

He steps in, a delicate foil-wrapped box cradled in his hands. I blink, startled, as he sets it on the bathroom counter and moves closer.

"I, uh... brought you something," he says, smiling in that gentle way that makes me melt. I can't help but meet it with a smile of my own.

"What is it?"

He nudges the box toward me. "Go on, open it."

I dry my hands with a plush towel before lifting the lid. Inside, nestled in crinkled tissue paper, rests a slim glass bottle of perfume. I couldn't quite pronounce the name, but I could tell it was expensive.

"Where did you get this?" I ask, glancing up.

Henry shrugs, looking almost boyish as he leans against the doorframe. "I was wandering after dinner, saw it in one of the resort's shops, and thought of you."

I pick up the bottle, a swirl of pale pink liquid glinting in the soft light behind the elegant label.

"It's beautiful," I say quietly. My fingertips brush over the top before I give a small spritz onto my wrist.

The scent rushes forward: sweet, soft rose layered over a darker undercurrent of musk. It's instantly warm and strangely familiar, tugging at my memory. A pang flutters in my chest—something about it sets every nerve on edge.

I inhale again, more deeply this time. Rose and musk. My heart clenches. Where have I smelled this before?

Then, like a flash of lightning on a dark horizon, it hits me.

Genevieve.

A sliver of confusion slices through me, followed immediately by a spike of dread. My mouth goes dry as I search Henry's gaze. Is this deliberate?

He smiles, stepping forward to brush a damp lock of hair from my forehead. "You like it?"

I swallow hard, forcing a nod. "Yeah," I manage, though my voice sounds distant to my own ears. "It's...I mean, it's lovely."

"Good," he says, relief evident in his tone. "I just wanted to do something nice for you. Especially after today."

A tremor works its way through me, but I keep my face as placid as I can. My mind is already spinning with questions, doubts, and the uncanny realization that the very essence of that *snake* is now on my skin. The bath's warmth feels suddenly stifling.

"Thank you," I say, inhaling slowly to keep my composure. "I really appreciate it."

He leans in, pressing a tender kiss to my temple. "I'll see you in bed, okay?"

I force a smile I can't feel.

"Sure," I whisper, clutching the perfume bottle close.

The scent clings to my skin, invading my senses, sinking into me.

Not mine.

Not his.

Hers.

SIXTEEN
HENRY

God, these counseling sessions are unbearable. They remind me of when my mother sent me to therapy as a boy, convinced I had anger issues. But that wasn't the real problem. The problem was that I was a young man going through puberty, hormones swinging wildly, and thanks to my parents, I had more money than sense.

Most people dream about what they'll do when they grow older—how they'll earn a living, spend their money, and find purpose.

Me? I never got to have that. I knew exactly what would happen. I'd inherit my father's wealth, his oil empire, his real estate, and continue to grow it as he did, just as his father had done before him. And when my days were finished, I'd pass it down to my child, expecting him to do the same.

Just to paint the picture more clearly, my first car was a Ferrari Superamerica. It sounds like something made up, but it's real, and it costs more than most people could ever dream of affording. And that was just the beginning.

I glance sideways at Morgan, suddenly curious what her first car might have been. Feeling the weight of my gaze, she turns and meets my eyes with that mesmerizing green stare that always seems to swallow me whole.

She's stunning—and she doesn't even know it.

The door opens, interrupting my thoughts, and Dr. Warren crosses the room, settling elegantly into her armchair.

"Apologies for keeping you waiting," she says calmly. "Shall we begin?"

"Please," I say, conscious that I've been drumming my fingers restlessly on the armrest.

Dr. Warren's eyes flick to my fingers, a slight crease forming between her brows. Not wanting her to analyze me too closely, I slow my movements, becoming deliberately precise. She shifts her gaze to Morgan instead, waiting expectantly.

Silence stretches heavily between us until Morgan finally clears her throat. "Am I supposed to speak?"

Dr. Warren smiles gently. "Yes, my dear. Why don't you start us off? How have things been since our last session?"

"Good," I answer quickly, almost automatically. I sense how uncomfortable Morgan is; she must hate these sessions as much as I do. I find her hand and give it a reassuring squeeze. "We're good."

"Are we?" Morgan's voice is so quiet I almost think I misheard. It's only when she looks at me, vulnerability shimmering in her eyes, that I realize she's serious.

Dr. Warren tilts her head slightly, curiosity lighting

her face. "Morgan, is there something you'd like to discuss?"

I can't tear my eyes away from Morgan as she takes a shaky breath, looking away from me as though afraid to hold my gaze.

"It's nothing major. Everything's fine, really. It's just..."

I brace myself, knowing exactly what name she's about to say, my jaw clenching in preparation.

"Genevieve."

Eve.

Dr. Warren repeats the name softly, jotting it down. "Tell me about her."

"She's someone we met here," I jump in, forcing my voice to remain neutral. I don't want Morgan to think I'm angry or defensive. "She recognized me from a long time ago. Like I said before, we barely know each other."

Dr. Warren nods slowly, then addresses Morgan. "How do you feel about Henry knowing someone here?"

Morgan shifts uneasily in her seat, gripping the fabric beneath her fingers. "I don't know. I just want to understand exactly what their relationship was. Henry keeps saying it's nothing, but it doesn't feel like nothing. I just want the truth."

A heavy sigh escapes me. I run my hand through my hair, frustration mounting. Why can't Morgan see I've already committed myself to her entirely? There's nothing to worry about.

"There's nothing, Morgan. Absolutely nothing. You have to trust me."

"If you really cared about me, you'd tell me the truth," she says, sharper than she probably intended.

I stare at her, incredulous. "I do care about you! That's exactly why I bought you the perfume."

Dr. Warren leans in slightly. "Perfume?"

"Yes, perfume. It was just a little gift. A nice gesture. Because I care about her, and I want her to feel special."

Dr. Warren's eyes shift to Morgan. "Morgan, did it make you feel special?"

Morgan looks down, visibly uncomfortable. "At first. But the perfume he gave me—it smells exactly like Genevieve."

"I didn't even know that! It was just the nicest perfume in the store. The most expensive, the most popular—"

Dr. Warren cuts in smoothly. "Henry, do you like the way Genevieve smells?"

My jaw drops. "Excuse me?"

"Answer the question."

My nostrils flare. "I don't care about her. I just liked the scent. Period."

"So you do."

My jaw ticks.

"Can you see why Morgan might feel unsettled by that?"

"It was an innocent mistake." I turn to Morgan, my voice softening. "You're letting her get into your head. She's not in this relationship—it's just you and me."

Morgan's voice lowers, barely audible. "I'm not obsessed. But she's not just some random woman. There's something more, Henry. I feel it."

A muscle ticks in my cheek as I look away. "There isn't."

"Then tell me." Her voice is desperate now. "If you care about me, just tell me the truth."

I lean back, shoulders sagging under the weight of things I can't say. Eve has always haunted me, even when I believed I was free. She won't stop until she ruins everything—especially my chance at happiness with Morgan.

"I've told you everything I know," I whisper.

Dr. Warren allows silence to gather before speaking again, thoughtful and measured. "Morgan, uncertainty is unsettling. Trust is delicate."

"You think I'm just being paranoid?" Morgan cuts in.

"No. I'm actually suggesting that perhaps your best course of action is direct confrontation—why not meet with Genevieve yourself? Get to know her better. Clear the air."

Morgan considers this suggestion thoughtfully, and I can see the resolve settle into her expression.

My stomach plummets. Dr. Warren's solution feels less like advice and more like an invitation to my worst nightmare. Morgan getting to know Eve directly?

I want to grind my teeth, tear out my hair. Every carefully hidden secret, every carefully buried lie—all teetering on the edge of exposure.

Instead, I force a smile, nodding weakly as Morgan agrees, even though every instinct I have screams in protest.

But it's too late. Truth be told, from the moment she set foot on the tarmac, she'd already slipped beneath our skin. And now there's nothing I can do but watch help-lessly as my world begins to crumble.

SEVENTEEN
MORGAN

While Henry's getting his miles in at the gym, I'm sitting at the poolside bar, clutching a passionfruit mocktail in one hand, a paperback balanced precariously in the other. I've stared at the same page for thirty minutes, rereading the same few sentences without absorbing a single word. My mind keeps drifting, stubbornly stuck on the one person I wish I could forget: Genevieve.

As much as I try to push her away, her presence keeps resurfacing, burrowing beneath my skin. I can't shake the image of her standing so confidently beside Henry, the intimate familiarity between them gnawing at my peace of mind.

Dr. Warren's suggestion still echoes in my head—meet with Genevieve and confront the issue head-on. It sounded good when I was seated in front of her, when it was just an idea. But now that I was out from the protection of that armchair, the very thought—I hate to say it, I really do—intimidates me.

It makes my stomach twist with anxiety, because I

was never good at confrontation. Growing up, whenever bullies took aim at me, I'd make myself small and just take it. Back then, it never felt worth the fight. I didn't have anything important enough to protect or care about. They mostly went after my books, and I knew that the few books they tore had plenty of copies.

But now, it's different.

Now, I have Henry.

And as much as I want to deny it, I'm terrified of losing him. Terrified that this woman from his past might take him from me—despite his insistence that there's nothing between them. The uncertainty has me tightly wound, anxious, wondering if it's paranoia or instinct.

I sigh heavily, setting my book down on the polished wooden surface of the bar, admitting defeat. My mocktail sits half-forgotten, a ring of condensation spreading beneath it.

"Something on your mind?"

I glance up sharply, jolted from my reverie by the bartender's gentle voice. He's smiling politely, eyes bright with casual interest as he wipes down the bar top.

"What makes you ask that?" I respond, slightly embarrassed, but grateful for a voice that wasn't my own, echoing around inside my head.

He chuckles softly, nodding toward the book lying face down. "You've been stuck on that same page for almost half an hour, and I know it's a good book."

I turn it over, glancing at the familiar cover with a sheepish smile. "That obvious, huh?"

"A little," he says with a sympathetic grin, polishing a

clean spot on the already immaculate bar top. "Want to talk about it? Or would you prefer another mocktail?"

"Maybe both," I concede with a faint laugh, pushing the glass toward him. "I'll take another passionfruit one."

"Coming right up." He sets to work, his movements practiced and efficient, filling the shaker with ice and juice. "Relationship troubles?"

"What makes you think that?"

He shrugs, an easy smile softening his features. "Bartender's intuition, I suppose. Most of the troubles people have here are relationship-related."

I laugh, "Then maybe you should get that intuition checked out. You're off the mark a little bit."

"Oh? So it's *not* relationship troubles?" he sounds curious now.

"More so *woman* troubles."

He chuckles, "Some of the other women here bothering you?"

"Just one, in particular. Maybe you know her? Genevieve... I don't even know her last name. But she's the hot one strutting around."

His eyes dart toward another member of staff walking by, his expression marked with a sudden nervousness. I imagine he's not really supposed to discuss the state of affairs with Eden guests. He could get fired if someone overheard.

But instead of sitting back, I lean in, a sly grin playing at my lips. "You *do* know who I'm talking about."

"Everyone on the island knows Genevieve. She's something of a... well, she's something."

"That's a light way to put it," I say with a soft laugh,

despite myself. I hesitate, fingers drumming against the bartop. What harm could come from opening up just a bit? "Supposedly she knows my husband, Henry. From before, I guess. He says they barely knew each other, but... I don't know."

He finishes pouring the shaken contents of the mocktail into a frosted glass and slides it in front of me. He leans in conspiratorially close, and his voice dips into a lower pitch.

"And it's bothering you."

He says it like a statement, not a question.

Eyeing him, I nod, and say, "The counselor thinks I should talk to her directly. Work it out with her."

"She would say something like that," he mutters.

I frown. "What's that supposed to mean?"

His eyes dart around again, like he's just realized he wasn't supposed to say that. He backs up a fraction, before leaning in and saying, "Look, you seem nice. Be careful with her. I mean it. She's not what she seems. *Nothing* is."

Footsteps sound behind him, and he jerks back like he's been shot. In the flash of an eye, he's got his cloth back in hand, wiping across the tabletop.

He dips his head at me with a forced smile and winks, "Enjoy the mocktail, Mrs. Langford."

Another member of staff—his boss?—appears over his shoulder and smiles at me.

"Thank you very much. You've been incredibly helpful."

He nods and starts to walk away.

"I didn't catch your name," I say, bringing him to a halt. His boss looks on at us with curiosity.

"My name is Luka."

"Well... this is the best passionfruit mocktail I've had in a long while, Luka," I say, swirling the melting ice in my glass. "I hope I'll see you around."

"I'm glad you like it. I'll be seeing you." He disappears into the back, leaving the boss to man the bar.

I lift the straw to my mouth, taking a slow sip as I stare across the shimmering turquoise water, trying to mask the sharp edge of fear tightening my chest.

What did he mean that Genevieve wasn't what she seemed? And why did I need to be careful of her?

A shuddering breath leaves me, unsteady, rattling through my ribs. The weight of Luka's words presses against my spine, a warning coiling in my gut. I need to clear my head.

Tucking the book under my arm, I pick up my drink and step off the pool deck, making my way toward the beach. The sand is warm beneath my feet, grounding me as I walk toward the water's edge. The ocean breeze wraps around me, lifting strands of my hair and carrying with it the crisp scent of salt and sun. It should be soothing. It should be enough to calm me.

But it isn't. Not after what I just heard.

A member of staff—someone with no reason to lie—just warned me.

That alone solidifies the thought already forming in my mind. Genevieve isn't just some woman from Henry's past.

She's here to take him from me.

Avoiding her won't change that. Avoiding her won't give me peace. If anything, it will only feed my paranoia, coil it tighter until it consumes me whole. Dr. Warren was right—if I wanted answers, if I wanted control over the situation, I needed to face her directly.

The tightness in my chest constricts, winding around my lungs. I sip my passionfruit mocktail, hoping the tartness will snap me back to reality, pull me out of the spiraling thoughts circling my mind like vultures.But the taste doesn't even register.

Because I can't shake her.

And now, more than ever, I refuse to believe that this is just jealousy or insecurity twisting me up inside. Maybe Henry *is* telling the truth. Maybe he barely knew her. But that doesn't mean Genevieve isn't a problem.

Fingers tap my shoulder. I glance back. A member of staff is standing behind me, holding a small, folded card. With a courteous nod, she offers it to me.

"A message, ma'am."

"Let me guess. From my Eden representative?" I ask as I take the card.

She shakes her head. "No, ma'am. This is from another guest of the resort who specifically asked that this be delivered to you."

I unfold the card. It's an invitation to a spa day.

And it's from *her*.

EIGHTEEN
MORGAN

Genevieve's invitation stares up at me from the glossy card sitting innocently on the table. The handwritten note is elegant and precise, each swirling letter a quiet taunt, daring me to confront her. I bite my lip, considering my options carefully.

Part of me still hears Luka's quiet, cautious voice echoing in my mind, telling me to be careful. But another part clings to Dr. Warren's calm, measured advice: confront the situation directly. Take control. Stop letting Genevieve try to pull the strings in the shadows of my marriage.

But was meeting her at the spa really the right move?

On one hand, a spa was neutral ground—calming, peaceful, maybe even reassuring. But on the other, it felt oddly vulnerable, almost too intimate. Maybe that was exactly why Genevieve had chosen it. Did she plan to soften me up, break down my defenses?

An alternative flashes through my mind: Decline the invitation and instead meet somewhere public, somewhere safer, somewhere I can regain control. Maybe a quiet café, or better yet, at the bar—where Luka could listen in, and give me his honest impression afterward.

I press my fingertips to my temple, feeling the sharp tension knotting beneath my skin. I roll my shoulders, trying to ease the tightness, but the dull ache persists stubbornly. My chiropractor's voice reminds me that scrunching my shoulders won't solve anything, but it's a habit I've yet to break.

The bathroom door opens abruptly, steam rolling out in thick clouds. Henry emerges, fresh from his shower, his hair damp and tousled.

My eyes catch on the taut muscles of his stomach, and warmth spreads through me. He catches me staring and gives me a smile that sends butterflies through my stomach.

I blush, but I don't look away. This wasn't just a boyfriend, or some stranger. No, this was my husband.

My perfect, dreamy husband.

He crosses the room and wraps his strong arms around me, his touch instantly comforting and reassuring. It helps to chase away some of the anxious shadows lingering in my chest.

God, I love him.

"How was your day?" he murmurs softly against my hair, pressing a gentle kiss to my temple.

I melt slightly, leaning into him, craving the security he offers.

"It was fine," I say quietly, not wanting to shatter this moment with my worries about Genevieve. "Just relaxed by the pool, tried to read."

"Tried?" Henry pulls back slightly, studying my face closely. "Everything okay?"

I glance up into his eyes, searching for any hint that he's hiding something, anything—but all I see is genuine concern and tender affection. Maybe I was right earlier in thinking that perhaps he *isn't* hiding anything.

"I'm fine," I say with a small, reassuring smile. "Just tired."

He nods slowly, studying my face closely, clearly sensing something deeper beneath my words. But he doesn't press. Instead, he pulls me closer, running a comforting hand up and down my back, soothing the tension lingering in my shoulders.

"Maybe we should go out tonight," he suggests softly, brushing his lips against my forehead again. "Dinner somewhere nice. Just the two of us."

"I'd like that." It feels good to focus on him again, to lose myself in Henry rather than my relentless doubts. Maybe that's exactly what I need—to step away from it all, even if just for an evening.

But then, from the corner of my eye, the invitation catches my gaze again, taunting me silently from where I'd placed it down on the dresser. Genevieve's invitation. My stomach twists sharply, anxiety seeping back into my veins.

Henry's voice is soft against my hair, oblivious to the turmoil swirling within me. "Perfect. I'll make a reservation at that place you liked the other night. The one on the water?"

"Sounds perfect."

Henry nods, raking a hand through damp hair as he

heads to the closet. I chew my lip, staring at the invitation in my hands, the beautiful writing taunting me.

"Hey, Henry?"

"Yeah?" he calls from inside, his voice slightly muffled.

I hesitate, gripping the card a little tighter. "I think I'm going to do a spa day tomorrow."

He pokes his head out, his smile easy. "That sounds like a great idea. Could be relaxing. Want me to come with you? We could do a couple's spa."

I hesitate, my fingers tracing over the lettering on the invitation. "Actually, I think I'll be doing it with Genevieve."

His smile vanishes in an instant, the warmth in his expression replaced by something sharp and tense. "What do you mean, you'll be doing it with her?"

I hold up the card. "She invited me."

His jaw tightens. "Don't tell me you're actually going through with what Dr. Warren suggested."

"I think I am, actually."

Henry crosses the room in three quick strides, then drops to his knees in front of me, gripping my hands like he's afraid I might slip away. There's something unnerving in the way he looks at me—like he's staring at the edge of a cliff, and I'm the one about to jump.

"Morgan, you don't need to do this," he says, his voice low, urgent. "You don't know her. You're *not* going to be fine."

I cup his cheek, my thumb brushing against the sharp line of his jaw. "Henry, you don't have to worry so much. I'm not walking into a war zone—I'm going to a spa."

His grip tightens. "Tell me you're not doing this to test me. To see if I've been lying about her."

I sigh, pressing a soft kiss to his lips, trying to ease the tension brimming beneath his skin. "Look, Henry. I believe you. I really do. But that doesn't mean I'm going to sit back and let her interfere in our relationship while we're here. I want to shut it down. Set boundaries. And who knows, maybe we can even get back on good terms."

Henry lets out a sharp, humorless laugh, pulling away. "Good terms? Morgan, there are no good terms with that woman."

I frown, studying his face carefully. "What aren't you telling me?"

He exhales through his nose, like he's weighing his next words carefully. Finally, he looks up at me, something raw and reluctant flickering in his eyes.

"Remember how in counseling, she recognized me from a long time ago?"

I nod slowly, a growing unease settling into my chest. "Yeah, you said you hardly knew each other."

"Well, that's not entirely true. We were childhood friends," he begins cautiously, running a tense hand down his face. "What's important for you to know is that Eve's crazy, Morgan. Actually crazy. She was institutionalized for a while—a psych ward."

A chill slips down my spine, but I force myself to hold steady, though my voice trembles slightly. "And you never thought to mention that?"

His gaze darkens, frustration coloring his expression. "Because I was trying to keep you away from her. There's a reason *I've* been steering clear of her."

His words hang between us, heavy with unspoken warning.

Suddenly, the spa invitation feels far less like an olive branch and far more like a trap. My fingers tighten around the card involuntarily.

"Oh," I whisper, unable to tear my gaze away from the elegant handwriting.

"Yeah," Henry replies softly.

Frustrated, I toss the invitation aside and bury my face in my hands, pressing my fingers against my temples. "Why didn't you mention this sooner, Henry? This is exactly the kind of thing you're supposed to share with your wife."

His laughter is short, bitter. "And what exactly was I supposed to say? 'Hey, my lovely darling wife of a few days, you see that girl over there? She's crazy, stay away from her.' Yeah, that would have gone great."

I groan, hating how reasonable he sounds, how right he probably is. There really wasn't an easy way for him to bring something like this up. If I were in his shoes, I probably would've tried to avoid the conversation altogether, hoping Genevieve stayed away on her own.

Still, something about all of this bothers me. Eden was supposed to be meticulous, thorough. So how did they miss something like this? Weren't they dedicated to ensuring their matches succeeded, striving for everlasting happiness? Putting Henry's unstable childhood friend on the same island during our honeymoon felt reckless, bordering on intentionally cruel.

"Promise me you won't meet her," Henry says suddenly, his voice soft and pleading, almost childlike.

My eyes find his, the worry in his gray gaze tugging at something deep inside me. With a heavy, resigned sigh, I nod slowly. "Okay."

Henry visibly relaxes, relief washing over his features as he leans forward, pressing a tender kiss to my forehead. "Thank you."

I manage a small smile, knowing full well I wasn't surrendering—merely shifting gears.

I stretch my arms over my head and roll my shoulders, trying to relieve the stubborn tension that's settled there.

"It's a shame. I was looking forward to the spa. I've never been able to afford the experience, so..."

His eyes soften. "I suppose you could still go, just at a different time than her?"

I pause. "You think?"

"Sure. I mean, could be helpful, give you some time alone to really unwind." He hesitates, then adds, "So long as you're definitely not meeting her."

"Yeah, no, I don't want to meet her." I run my hands through my hair, aware of how it could do with some treatment after my time in the ocean. "Alright. Maybe I'll do it. After all, things have been... a lot lately."

At least that part isn't a lie.

His shoulders relax further, a smile finally returning. He presses a kiss to my head. "Good. You deserve a break. Take some time for yourself."

"Yeah, I really do," I echo softly, convincing myself as much as him.

But beneath my calm exterior, my thoughts race. If Eve is truly as unstable as Henry claims, then sitting back passively would only empower her. Letting her slink around unchecked, weaving herself deeper into our lives, would be the real danger. No. I couldn't allow that. I had to do something proactive, something *decisive*. I needed clear boundaries set firmly and unmistakably.

As Henry retreats into the closet to finish dressing, I cross the room quickly, reaching for the landline phone on the bedside table. My hand trembles slightly as I dial, my voice carefully casual as someone answers immediately.

"Could you please get in touch with my Eden representative, Dexter? I need to meet with him as soon as possible," I say, sounding far calmer than I feel.

There's a brief pause before the polite but firm reply. "I'm sorry, Mrs. Langford, but Mr. Dexter is currently off-island. He'll return in the next few days. Would you like me to leave a message?"

Frustration and disappointment surge through me, tightening my grip on the phone. I force my voice to remain steady. "No, that's fine. I'll reach out again once he's back."

"Of course. Enjoy your evening, Mrs. Langford."

I slowly hang up, the quiet click of the receiver echoing in the silence of the room. Dexter's absence means I'm completely on my own, at least for now. A sense of urgency tightens in my chest. I couldn't afford to wait days for him to return. Who knew what kind of damage Genevieve could cause in that time.

My gaze shifts once again to the invitation lying discarded on the nightstand. Her elegant writing mocks me from under the lamplight. Henry might think he'd convinced me to stay clear of Eve, but I knew better than to simply ignore a threat like her.

She wants to meet? To play her games, to sink her claws into the one thing I've spent my life longing for?

Fine. Let's play.

Let's see who comes out on top.

NINETEEN

MORGAN

The resort spa is beyond anything I could have imagined.

Stepping inside, I'm momentarily stunned by the sheer beauty of it—the cascading water features, the faint scent of jasmine and eucalyptus drifting through the air, the soft golden lighting that makes the space feel both intimate and impossibly luxurious. The floors are a cool, polished stone, the walls lined with elegant wooden panels and intricate carvings. Everything is curated for relaxation, designed to lull guests into a sense of ease.

And as much as I can't afford to settle into ease, I find myself breathing in deeply, letting the spa's tranquil atmosphere settle around me. For a brief moment, I let myself believe that I came here just for this—for the warmth of the sauna, the weightlessness of a deep soak, the indulgence of an expert massage.

I let the receptionist guide me through the process, handing me a robe as she speaks in a soft, melodic voice about the services available.

My body moves on autopilot, nodding at all the right

moments, my mind holding tight to Henry's warning. I had to remember, this wasn't a haven of peace. This was a battleground with someone who was legitimately crazy.

After slipping into the changing area, I undress, folding my clothes neatly in the locker before wrapping myself in the plush, cloud-like robe provided.

The first treatment—a heated stone massage—melts away some of the tension lodged deep in my muscles, coaxing me into a momentary sense of surrender.

Maybe Henry was right. Maybe I did need this.

But then, as I make my way back into the main relaxation area, my stomach knots.

There, draped across one of the cushioned treatment tables, is Genevieve.

She lounges nearly naked, a pristine white towel draped over her hips. Her eyes are closed in serene relaxation, like she's asleep, leaving me free to study her long and toned limbs.

Her skin is smooth and perfect. There's not even a single strand of hair on her—not on her legs, not on her arms, not anywhere.

Self-consciously, I glance down at my own legs, breathing a curse as I wish I'd shaved before I came.

"You came."

Her voice is lazy, pleased, like she expected me all along. Like this was never my decision, but hers.

The air between us thickens, the tranquility of the spa twisting into something else entirely.

And just like that, I know the game's begun.

I settle onto the table beside her, shifting awkwardly as I try to get the towel to lay just right. The fabric clings in all the wrong places, making me hyper-aware of every inch of exposed skin.

Genevieve cracks an eye open, amusement flickering across her face. A soft chuckle escapes her lips.

"We're the only ones here, Morgan. No need for modesty."

I grunt in response, determined to keep at least one layer of distance between us. The last thing I need is for Genevieve to see my hoo-ha. Some things, no matter how luxurious the setting, are non-negotiable.

Once I finally get the towel to sit properly, I exhale, sinking my head back against the plush pillow. The silence stretches between us, taut like a rope waiting for one of us to pull too hard and snap it.

I should be the one to speak first. I should take control, set the tone, lay down the boundaries I came here to establish. But frustratingly, a small part of me—one I wish I could smother—hesitates, waiting to see where she wants to take this.

Because what if, a tiny voice whispers, she didn't bring you here to play games? What if this isn't a power move, but an olive branch like you thought before? What if she just wants to make peace?

"Morgan," she says finally, her voice smooth as warmed honey. "I think we got off on the wrong foot."

I let out a breath, almost laughing at the wave of relief. It actually sounds like she's trying to make amends. A small smile tugs at my lips.

"I think you might be right."

She sighs, stretching her arms above her head like a cat in the sun. "I didn't expect to run into Henry here, of all places. And certainly not with Brody. I'm sure you can appreciate how... awkward that is."

"It's weird, isn't it?" I say, something easing in my shoulders.

Maybe it's the spa's thick, fragrant steam, or maybe it's the fact that this is going way better than I expected, but for the first time since arriving, I feel the tension in my spine start to unravel. Who knows? Maybe this will just be a relaxing spa day after all.

"Eden is supposed to be super thorough," I continue, the words coming easier now. "They interviewed me with a *polygraph*, but somehow they let this happen? They missed something this big?"

Genevieve smiles, but says nothing. Her eyes remain closed, her expression unreadable. Something about it worries me.

"How's Brody?" I ask, searching for neutral ground.

She waves a hand lazily through the air, the movement fluid and effortless, like she's swatting at something unimportant. Like *he's* unimportant.

Something about it puts a pause in me.

Maybe this isn't going to go as well as I thought.

"Let's talk about Henry instead," she says, tilting her head slightly toward me, her voice syrupy smooth. "How are things between you two?"

As much as I don't want to discuss him with her, maybe flaunting how strong we are will put her off— make her see there's no chance of tearing us apart.

"Really great, honestly. It's everything I dreamed of when I signed up for Eden, and Henry says the same. It's kind of a perfect match."

"Is that so?" Her voice is deadpan, but I catch the tiniest flicker of something in her expression—annoyance, disappointment? It's bad, but a thrill runs through me. A guilty pleasure at the fact that, for once, someone else wants what *I* have.

"It is," I say, stretching out against the table, feigning ease.

"Have you ever wondered why you were chosen for him?"

"You mean why Eden paired us up?" I shrug. "We've got all the matching qualities, desires in life, you know."

"Oh, I have no doubt that you're exactly what he wanted."

"What do you mean?"

"Let me guess. You have no friends, no family, no career aspirations. You're a nobody who desperately wants to be with somebody." She lifts a finger, like she's cutting me off before I can say anything. "And now, you are. You're with the *perfect* man, aren't you?"

My nostrils flare as I try to control my anger. I hate that she managed to cut so deep so easily, seeing me for what I am. But I still have the one thing she wants. "I am with the perfect man, and he's all mine."

Genevieve exhales through her nose, long and tedious, then closes her eyes. "Nobody's perfect, Morgan. You should be careful."

"You think I should be careful of my own husband?"

She hums, lazy, like this is all just conversation. "I know him better than you think. He has anger issues, did you know that? His mother even sent him to therapy when he was younger."

I hesitate. Henry never mentioned anything like that to me.

"It was a big to-do, but look at him now. Maybe it worked."

"I didn't know about that," I mutter.

"There's a lot you don't know about him. Or me. Really, we're all just strangers at the end of the day, aren't we?"

I steel myself. "I know a couple of things about you."

She smirks, amused. "Do please share."

"No judgment," I say with a slow shrug. "I think we all had our issues when we were younger. But Henry did mention you were committed. Or something like that?"

The reaction is immediate. Her shoulders tighten. One of the towels slips from where it was tucked, landing on the floor with a soft thump. Slowly, deliberately, she sits up, letting the other towel fall away as well. The sudden wave of steam from the spa obscures her just enough, but I still see more than I want to. More than I need to.

A wave of jealousy rolls through me at just how impossibly stunning she is. It makes my stomach twist, because I know exactly what she's doing—taunting me, trying to remind me that she's better than me. And clearly, she thinks that means she should have her hands on my husband.

But that just wasn't going to happen.

Despite myself, despite the anxiety clawing at my stomach, I sit up too. I let my towel fall away, hoping the steam does me the same favor it does her, covering what I don't want her to see.

Her gaze flicks over me, assessing, before she leans back on her hands, tilting her head slightly. "You think you know Henry?"

"I do," I say firmly. "I know that he's the best thing that's ever happened to me."

"Sure." Her smile is lazy, stretching over her lips.

"Certainly the best thing to happen to me in bed, that's for sure." Somewhere, some past version of me gasps as how vicious I'm being. But I have to be this way if I want her to back off.

She raises an eyebrow and stares at me, wearing that cold, unfeeling expression again. I know I've caught her off guard with the comment.

"I didn't know you were such a slut, Morgan."

I actually laugh, unbothered by her comment. "I was a virgin, actually. Gladly. Until Henry." I pause, letting it sink in. "He's... voiced his pleasure about it."

Something in her jaw ticks. It's subtle, but I catch it. And the look in her eyes makes me wonder—just for a moment—if I've pushed too far. The conversation has taken a turn, the kind that doesn't end well for either of us.

I clear my throat and decide to cut through the tension. "Look, I get it. You and Henry have some sort of distant history. That's great. It's always nice to see old friends. But I have to draw the line here. Henry and I just got married. You need to give us space."

She rolls her tongue over her teeth, gaze sharp as a blade as she watches me. In that moment, I see it—the instability lurking beneath the surface, the barely concealed edge of something dangerous. A bead of sweat slips down my temple, but for the first time, I hold my ground.

"Maybe it'll be good for you and Brody too," I add, doing everything I can to keep from shaking and to keep my voice steady. "He seems like a genuinely good guy. I'm sure he'd like that."

A heavy silence falls between us, stretching long enough that I start to regret speaking at all. Then, suddenly, she stands. One slow, deliberate step forward, until I'm forced to tilt my chin up to meet her gaze.

There's something undeniably unnerving about a naked woman standing this close, looking like she's debating whether or not to kill you.

She draws a breath, then hesitates. Her nostrils flare slightly, and her gaze flickers over me. I realize, with no small amount of satisfaction, that she's smelling the perfume Henry bought me—the blend of rose and musk he picked out just for me. I wore it on purpose, bearing a silent message: *he's mine.*

Her lips part slightly, but then she exhales, smoothing a hand over her face. When she speaks again, her voice is softer, lighter. "Maybe you're right. I have the tendency to be catty, and perhaps I've been... overstepping."

She steps back, perching on the edge of her table again, as if the moment never happened.

I narrow my eyes. Waiting for the catch.

She offers a languid smile, softer now. "Brody is a good man. I'm just adjusting to him. It's a process, which I'm sure you can... appreciate."

I don't believe her, not for a second. But I nod anyway. "That's good."

A pause, then she says, "Let's do something nice. A fresh start?"

In a tentative voice, I ask, "Like what?"

Her gaze flicks to my hair, and then she smiles. "You have beautiful hair, you know. But haven't you ever wanted to do something with it?"

Instinctively, my fingers comb through the strands, still tangled from the salt air. Truth be told, I've considered changing it, but I never knew what I wanted.

She watches me carefully, then presses on, her voice coaxing. "Let's have the staff do our hair. I need a little refresh myself. And I might have some ideas for you."

I hesitate, something about this—about her—making me wary. But then she twinkles her fingers at me, almost teasing. "Come on. A little change. It'll be refreshing, I promise."

It's small. Harmless. And my hair really could use some attention. I glance at my reflection in the polished chrome fixtures—worn, windblown, ends frayed from too many ocean swims.

"Alright," I say finally, feeling some of the tension in my shoulders release. Maybe, for once, she's being genuine. Maybe this is her way of making peace.

She smiles, signaling to the staff. "I think you'll love it."

I brace myself, waiting for the moment things will inevitably go wrong. But instead, the remainder of my spa experience turns out to be shockingly... pleasant.

We talk. We laugh, albeit cautiously. And when we finally step out, freshly polished and styled, looking better than ever, she pulls me into a hug. Like we're friends.

The idea of being actual friends with someone like her is unbearable. But for the first time, I wonder if we don't have to be enemies either.

I should've known better.

TWENTY

HENRY

I sink into the warm sand, panting lightly from the long swim I just finished. My lungs burn in that good way, the way that says, *You did something right.*

This is *life*. The sun overhead, the soft hush of waves, the salty breeze brushing my skin. For a second, I let my head tip back and close my eyes, exhaling a rush of satisfaction.

Everything's going to be okay now that I have Morgan. We'll figure this out. We'll build the kind of life I always wanted—one I never thought I'd be lucky enough to find.

"Henry!"

I hear her voice, like the call of an angel. And when I shift in the sand, shielding my eyes from the glare of the sun with a lifted hand, I see her.

Morgan is striding confidently across the beach in a black swimsuit I've never seen before, the kind that hugs every inch of her. She's got a big smile on her face, and it looks like her skin is glowing.

My heart thumps hard and fast at the sight of her. God, she's breathtaking. No, she's *radiant*.

Then, as she gets closer, I notice the swimsuit isn't the only thing new about her.

Her hair—

My stomach twists sharply at the sight. Her hair is woven into an intricate crown braid, looping elegantly around her head before cascading into a polished fishtail down her back. I haven't seen the style in years, but I remember it far too well.

Eve.

She wore it that first time I'd seen her, when we were just children standing in our parents' shadows as they tried to introduce us. Her hair had been done exactly like that.

I swallow, a chill crawling over my skin despite the heat. A dull ache starts to form in my chest.

She lied. Morgan *lied* to me.

My fingers curl into fists and my jaw ticks as I struggle to reconcile with the fact that my wife looked me in the face and *lied*.

"Hey," she says, dropping onto the sand next to me. She spins her head to the side so I can get the full view, looking more excited than I'd ever seen her, with one exception—the day we got married. "What do you think?"

She looks back at me, expecting the usual flood of compliments. But when she meets my eyes, the excitement dancing in her eyes starts to die down.

She cocks her head, eyebrows furrowing. Then her expression wavers.

"You don't like it?"

She must've seen the anger. The frustration. I open my mouth telling myself to say something, to say *anything*, but nothing comes out.

"You don't." Her voice falls flat, and she looks away, a deep frown creasing her face.

It pains me to see her hurting. So what if she lied and met with Eve? Maybe it went better than I imagined.

But deep down, I know that's not true. The truth is right here in front of me. Eve was leaving me a message.

I press my hand over Morgan's, drawing her attention back to me. "Sorry, it was just... unexpected."

She runs a hand over her hair. "I wanted to do something different."

"Let me guess. Eve suggested it."

She freezes.

"Morgan," I whisper, my voice barely carrying over the soft crash of the surf, "you told me you weren't going to—"

"I said I wouldn't meet her, but I changed my mind. I had to see her, Henry. She's been out of control lately, and... well, now it's all handled." Morgan looks me in the eye with a sly smile. "*I* handled it. We're on good terms now. She's the one who suggested this new hairstyle for me, and I think it looks great."

My heart sinks further. She really doesn't know how badly Eve's played her.

"Morgan... can you just stay away from her? Please?" My voice dips lower, and I know I sound desperate. "For me?"

She frowns, "Why?"

"That hairstyle..." I stop, swallowing hard. "I've seen it before."

Morgan's eyes widen, her lips parting in confusion. "What do you mean, you've seen it?"

I drag a hand across my face, unable to stop the unwelcome memory from flashing behind my eyes. "Eve wore her hair like that when we were kids. The first time I saw her, I mean... that was the exact style."

For a moment, Morgan just stares, and I can practically see the gears turning in her head.

"Oh," she finally breathes. "So she... oh." Her voice trembles with anger. "So she styled me like herself? Is that it?"

I nod reluctantly, the words tangling in my throat. "I don't know why, but... yes."

Morgan's fury flares in an instant. She starts tearing at her hair, screaming with unbridled rage. Her voice carries, drawing the attention of nearby couples and staff.

Worried, I reach for her hand, but she bats it away with a furious slap that leaves my hand stinging with pain.

"Don't touch me!" she shouts.

"Morgan!"

She jabs a finger into my chest, "What is this? Who *is* she to you?"

I stumble over the words, trying to formulate an answer that could fix all of this.

"How does she know so much about you, Henry?"

I look up at her. "What?"

"How does she know you were sent to therapy? To *anger management?*"

My forehead pinches. She told her that? She *actually* told her that? God, what a *snake*.

"It's obvious that you two were close. Your families were friends, right? She told me you've known each other forever—that you were practically raised together."

"We were close once," I admit, my voice low. "Our parents had businesses together. It was expected we'd see each other all the time. But it's not like that anymore."

Morgan's eyes flash, fury burning hotter with every breath. A staff member approaches, no doubt ready to suggest we take our marriage dispute somewhere more appropriate—probably to a counselor's office, where we'd bicker in those ridiculous chairs under the eye of that even more ridiculous woman.

But I fix him with a sharp look. He hesitates mid-step, reconsiders. Good. If I want to handle this here, on my terms, then that's exactly what I'm going to do.

"Why is she still so obsessed with you, Henry?"

I look away. I don't have an answer for her. God, I wish I did.

"And why does everyone keep warning me to be careful around her?"

"Everyone?" My gaze snaps back to hers. "Who else has said that?"

But she's not listening.

"You keep dropping half-truths, giving me pieces instead of the whole damn picture. What's the story between you two?" She draws a breath, chest rising sharply. "I love you, Henry."

"I love you too. I—"

"But I can't do this. Not with her always in the

picture like this. I don't even know who she really is to you. You have to tell me, or this isn't going to work."

My pulse hammers as panic claws up my throat. I can't lose her. Morgan is everything I've ever wanted, everything I've spent the last few years dreaming of. If she leaves...

"She's nothing to me except the absolute *bane* of my existence," I say, voice tight. "She's always there, always *has* been, and I can't get rid of her. I don't know why."

Morgan's expression sharpens. "What are you saying?"

I don't answer. A singular thought forms in my mind, eclipsing everything else.

I need a cigarette.

The need is instant, all-consuming. I turn away, rummaging through my things. I toss aside my shirt, the sunscreen, digging through the mess. Where the hell is it?

"Henry," Morgan says, voice strained.

I ignore her. I need that cigarette.

Sand scatters beneath my hands as I search.

"Henry," she says again, softer this time. I glance up to find her holding out the pack.

I snatch it from her hands, withdraw a cigarette, and flick a lighter to life. The first inhale sends nicotine rushing through my veins, a balm to the adrenaline tearing through me. Still, my hands shake, the burning ash dusting the golden sand.

"Is she a stalker?"

I look at Morgan. Her eyes are filled with concern.

"You said she was institutionalized. But you never told me why." A pause. "Was it because of you?"

Her voice trembles. It kills me. I rake a hand through my wet hair, struggling for words that won't make this worse. "I didn't think I'd ever see her again."

"Well, we have," she snaps, tears shining in her eyes. "And now she's trying to make me look like her? What is *wrong* with her?"

"I don't know," I say honestly, desperation creeping in. "But I'm sorry. This is exactly what I wanted to avoid."

She shakes her head and looks out over the ocean, silent for a long moment. Then, softly, she asks, "Is there anything else I need to know, Henry? If so... now's the time."

My heart twists. I wish I had easy answers—clean, simple truths that would fix everything. But nothing about Eve was ever simple.

I reach for Morgan's hand. "There's nothing else. She's more than just crazy. I... I'm sorry she's set her sights on you."

Morgan sighs, her new hairstyle falling around her face—an elegant, cruel reminder of Eve's presence.

"It's fine," she says, voice raw. "I've asked the staff to get me in touch with my Eden representative. Once Dexter's back, I'll have him deal with this. Maybe get us off this island, and back out there to real life. The sooner, the better."

I squeeze her hand, but she stands, slipping from my grasp.

"Are we okay?" I ask. I hate how vulnerable I sound, but this—this is what marriage is. Trusting someone enough to let them see the cracks.

Morgan exhales, nods. "Yeah. Just... don't hide anything else from me. Don't do it ever again."

I nod, swallowing the knot in my throat.

She offers a small, placating smile. "Don't worry, Henry. I'm not going to let her destroy what we have. No matter how hard she tries."

But even as she says it, I know it's a promise she may not be able to keep. And since I can't control my wife, I can only hope that she's up to the challenge.

TWENTY-ONE

MORGAN

I wait outside the door of the counseling session while Dr. Warren finishes with Henry. My reflection stares back at me in the mirror, and all I can think about is how Genevieve manipulated me.

How obsessed do you have to be to give someone your haircut just so it would remind their husband of you as a child?

Truth be told, I wanted to cut it all off. Shave my head. Enter my bald era. But Henry talked me out of it—not that he had to try very hard. I'd never gone that short before, and the idea scared me more than I cared to admit.

Besides, deep down, I knew the truth. As much as I hated to admit it, the hairstyle looked beautiful on me. When I left that spa, I thought *this is it*. I finally felt beautiful. And I know that even Henry thought so.

I sigh and force myself to look away from the mirror. It's frustrating how long they're taking with him. Maybe Henry has more issues to work through than I realized.

Maybe they know about his history with anger management and want to be absolutely sure he's in control. Who knows? But what I do know is that Dr. Warren has never once pulled me into a session of my own.

Maybe I should be grateful for that. The woman unnerves me.

Besides, I have bigger things to worry about. Any second now, I expect to hear footsteps echoing down the hallway, followed by the sharp click of Genevieve's heels. I can already picture her cold, assessing eyes slicing into me, that awful smirk tugging at the corner of her mouth.

But then the door opens.

Henry steps out, looking haggard and drained. And there's still no sign of her.

That surprises me. Genevieve and Brody's counseling sessions have always followed ours like clockwork.

Maybe she changed the timing to avoid confrontation.

The thought is almost laughable. *Avoid confrontation?* Please. That woman lives for it. And the idea that she'd willingly give up an opportunity to come face to face with my husband?

Even funnier.

Henry's eyes catch mine, and I realize whatever happened in his session took a lot out of him. He forces a weak smile, his hand rubbing the back of his neck.

I could tell he was itching for a cigarette.

"Everything okay?" I ask softly, stepping forward to lace my fingers into his, my other hand wrapping around his bicep in an attempt to comfort him.

"Yeah, just a long session."

"Did something happen?"

"No, just lots of questions. Lots and lots of questions." He gives me a sideward glance. "I am surprised, though."

"About what?"

"I thought you would bring Eve up whenever we were in there together. Talk about what she did to you."

A wave of exhaustion rolls through me, and I realize how *tired* I am of all this. Just a short while ago, I was desperate to be married, desperate to have the perfect husband. And now I *do*, and don't get me wrong, I'm beyond happy.

I just wish that he didn't come with baggage—the baggage being a stalker that's both stunning and crazy at the same time.

"No, there's no point in bringing that up. Those counseling sessions with Dr. Warren are for us, for the future of our marriage. This issue with Genevieve? That's between me and her."

He presses a kiss against the top of my head and we continue walking out of the building. My shoulders are tense, and for some reason, I feel irritated. Then, I realize why.

He said *Eve* again.

We step outside, leaving the sterile halls behind us. I pause, pulling him to a halt. He looks at me with those perfect, grey eyes.

"Morgan?"

"You know," I say, carefully choosing my words. "I'm still wondering why you keep calling her Eve. Her name's Genevieve."

Henry blinks, as if the thought has genuinely never occurred to him. "I—I don't know. It's just...habit, I guess. I've called her Eve since we were kids."

"Maybe it's time you stopped," I say softly but firmly, looking directly into his eyes. "It's part of moving on, isn't it? Reclaiming our lives, creating some distance?"

He swallows visibly, nodding with a solemn expression. "You're right. I'll stop. *Genevieve.*"

"Thank you," I say, squeezing his hand reassuringly. "It might seem small, but it means something to me."

We walk in silence for a while, making our way back toward the suite. I rest my head on Henry's shoulder, breathing in the salty ocean air. I'm not sure how long we were supposed to stay on the island, but it doesn't matter. Whenever Dexter gets back, that will be the end of it.

And as crazy as this place has been—with *her* here—I know, deep down, I'll miss it. After all, this is where I met Henry for the first time. Where we made love. Where we started something.

Couples stroll past, hands entwined, their faces bathed in the soft glow of lantern light. They smile at us, easy and genuine, and we smile back. The tension from the session with Dr. Warren fades, dissolving into the air. Warmth seeps back into my chest.

I trail my fingers along Henry's bare forearm, and he looks down at me, grinning. He's starting to recognize my tells. I return his smile, heat flushing my face with anticipation.

Then his expression shifts.

His gaze flickers past me, his grin faltering.

I turn to follow it.

Genevieve sits alone at the bar, her fingers curled delicately around a wine glass, swirling the deep red liquid as though she has all the time in the world.

She's staring right at us.

And her hair is in the same style she'd tricked me into wearing.

It's not a coincidence.

Henry exhales, shoulders tight, like just seeing her knocked the breath from his lungs. I feel the warmth drain out of me too, replaced by a fierce, burning hate.

"Listen," I say, tightening my grip on his arm. *Possessive*. "I'll see you back at the suite."

His jaw flexes. For a moment, I think he'll refuse, to insist on coming with me—absolutely not—or demand I go with him instead. But as much as I want to, I know it's time I had another conversation with Genevieve.

Maybe I wasn't clear enough the last time.

At last, Henry gives a hesitant nod. "Be careful," he murmurs, lifting my hand to his lips and pressing a soft kiss against my knuckles. It's protective. Maybe even pleading. "Please, Morgan."

I manage a small smile. "Always am."

Releasing his hand feels harder than it should, like I'm stepping away from safety. And in a way, I am. But this time, I don't care.

As we move forward, Genevieve doesn't look away. She watches us with those unhinged eyes, and I wonder how I ever missed how crazy she is.

I hate that we have to pass her to get to the suite. I hate that she gets to be close to him. Maybe she planned it that way—Brody nowhere in sight, sitting here *alone* so that she'd see Henry when we left Dr. Warren's office.

Her gaze flicks from me to him, and something shifts.

It's like a switch flips. The tension in her face softens, and a slow smile tugs at her lips.

"Henry," she purrs, her voice warm, low. Intimate.

I feel his whole body tense beside me.

"E—Genevieve," he says stiffly.

I squeeze his hand, trying to send him a silent message: *Don't acknowledge the psycho.*

But then—something unexpected happens.

At the sound of her full name, Genevieve flinches, recoiling like she's been struck.

Her expression twists with hurt. *Real* hurt.

A sharp thrill of satisfaction zips through me, and suddenly, I feel a surge of confidence.

I slide into the empty seat beside her as Henry walks away, passing all those happy, oblivious couples with no idea of the tension crackling like static here.

I signal to the bartender, and when he turns, I'm pleased to see it's Luka.

"Passionfruit mocktail?" he asks, his eyes flicking toward Genevieve. There's a warning there. I ignore it. I can handle her.

That look on her face—the wounded, vulnerable look—tells me something important.

She can be hurt.

And anything that can be hurt... can be *crushed*.

"Yes, please," I say, then turn to Genevieve. She's still watching Henry's retreating form like he's the only thing in the world.

I tilt my head.

"So," I ask, my voice smooth and sharp as a knife. "What *is* wrong with you?"

Even though I expect anger when she finally looks at me, I'm wholly unprepared for the sheer, unfiltered *hatred* burning in her eyes.

Her fingers tighten around the edge of the bar, nails digging into the wood, scraping slow, deliberate lines. Like she's imagining dragging them down my throat.

And for a second—a single, breathless second—I think she *might* actually do it.

But then, just as quickly, it's gone.

The moment flickers out like a snuffed flame, her face smoothing into something eerily composed. If not for the fresh gouges carved into the bar, I might have convinced myself I imagined the whole thing.

"Wrong with me?" she echoes softly, almost amused. A slow smile plays at the corner of her lips, unsettling and sharp. "Oh, Morgan. You're asking the wrong questions."

A chill slides down my spine, but I shove it back and square my shoulders.

"Am I?" I tilt my chin up. "Because from the moment you set foot on this resort, you've *completely* ignored your husband—who, I might add, is nowhere to be seen—and have been obsessed with *mine.*"

I hold up my hand, letting the sunlight catch the diamond on my finger.

"Do you see this ring? *He belongs to me.*"

Genevieve laughs—a light, airy sound that cuts deeper than any insult. It's the laugh of someone who isn't threatened in the slightest. It's the laugh of someone who doesn't even recognize my claim as real.

"Obsessed?" she murmurs, swirling her wine, watching the deep red liquid spin. "Of course I am."

My pulse spikes. Anger burns under my skin, igniting every nerve, but I can't think of a single thing to say. I just sit there, blood roaring in my ears, and it only seems to amuse her more.

Her smile stretches, slow and predatory, like she's savoring the exact moment she sees me start to slip.

She leans in, pressing her hand over mine.

"I *should* be obsessed, Morgan." She draws the words out, savoring every syllable. Then she drops it. *"I'm his wife."*

The world stops.

The chatter of the couples behind warps into static. The music fades. The air turns too thick to breathe.

My heart slams against my ribs, then drops straight into my stomach.

"What?" The word barely makes it out. Strangled. Hollow.

Genevieve rises smoothly from her stool, leaning in just enough that her perfume—*my perfume*—encloses me like a fog. My stomach churns. Our hair is the same. Our scent is the same. But in this moment, I feel like a pale imitation of her.

"*You heard me.*" Her voice is soft, but there's no warmth in it. Only satisfaction. "I'm Henry's wife."

I open my mouth, but nothing comes out.

Genevieve steps back, her lips curling like she's

already won. Then, without another word, she turns and walks away, heels clicking against the ground.

I don't move.

I don't breathe.

I just sit there, spiraling.

Because as much as I *want* to believe she's lying...

I'm no longer sure she is.

TWENTY-TWO

MORGAN

I'm still reeling when I step into the suite. My reflection in the mirror stops me cold—I'm pale, paler than I've ever seen myself. Like I've just seen a ghost.

Because maybe I *have*.

Genevieve's words echo in my head: "*I'm his wife.*"

Why would she say that? Is she really so twisted, so completely unhinged, that she's convinced herself Henry belongs to her?

My stomach lurches.

Or worse—what if it's not just in her head?

Henry emerges from the dressing room, wearing swim trunks and tugging a tank top into place. He freezes the second he sees me, his eyes darting over my face.

"What happened?" he asks, voice cautious, like he already knows something's wrong.

For a long, weighted moment, I can't speak. I just stare at him, searching for any flicker of cruelty, any sign he might be lying. But the longer I look, the more I hate how *perfect* he seems. How his eyes brim with kindness, how his body radiates strength, how everything about him screams safety.

Yet the doubt is there now—planted like a poison seed, thanks to a psychotic woman who won't let him go.

I sink into the nearest chair. Did Eden mess up? Give me a man who's separated, but still legally tied to someone else? The thought alone makes me want to vomit. The idea of Henry touching her—*kissing* her—makes bile rise in my throat.

I feel the nausea coming and bolt for the bathroom, shoving Henry aside. I gag over the sink, my stomach heaving, suddenly wishing I had my phone so that I could at least look it all up and put myself out of misery.

But almost immediately, Henry is behind me, pressing a comforting hand between my shoulder blades, drawing slow, soothing circles.

"Morgan," he says, voice tense with concern. "What's wrong?"

Tears blur my vision. I lift my gaze to his in the mirror.

"She said," I choke out, "she's your wife."

His face goes rigid, tension settling in his shoulders.

"Oh my god," I stammer, tears streaming. I slap his hand away, stumbling backward until my spine connects with the wall. "It's true, isn't it?"

He lifts both hands, like he's trying to show me he's unarmed, and the look he gives me is heartbreaking. "Look, Morgan. It's not what you think."

"Not what I think?" I scream, voice cracking. My nails dig into my scalp, tugging frantically at my hair, yanking it loose in uneven chunks, my breathing ragged and wild.

Then I spin, rip open the shower door, and step in with my clothes still on, like I can wash her scent off me. The scent Henry bought for me.

What kind of twisted man does that?

What kind of twisted *marriage* am I in?

"Morgan!" Henry shouts, ripping open the door.

To my shock, there are tears in his eyes. Maybe he thought he'd never have to tell me, and now that he's caught, he's devastated. Or maybe he hates that Eve still has control over him, that no matter how far he runs, she's still there, poisoning everything.

Whatever it is, I find myself backing away, my pulse pounding, my chest tightening with the overwhelming urge to leave. I want to go home. I want my library, my bus, my little apartment. I want to be far, far away from him and that *psycho* of a wife.

I rip the ring off my finger, ready to throw it at him, but he lifts his hands, desperate.

"Wait!" He steps into the shower after me, water pouring over both of us, his hair dripping down over his forehead. "I'm trying to tell you—it's not what you think."

I laugh, sharp and hollow. "Then what is it, Henry? How could this possibly be anything different than what I think?"

His jaw tightens, muscles ticking as he exhales through his nose. "I told you she was committed when we were younger, didn't I?"

I nod, my chin trembling as I fight to keep my heart from shattering completely.

"You already know she's obsessed with me, that she has... issues with stalking me. But what you don't know is that in *her* mind, she really does believe she's my wife. She's convinced we've been married since the moment she first laid eyes on me."

The ring wavers between my fingers. My brows furrow as I try to process his words, but when the meaning finally clicks, I lift my gaze to his, searching him for the truth.

"You're saying you're not actually...married?"

"God, no! We're not," he says, voice raw with frustration. "But she still *thinks* we are. It's been an issue for a long time."

The pieces start to fit. I've wondered how a man like Henry—with his wealth, his looks, his kindness—could possibly be single. Women would be lining up for him.

So why would someone like him need to sign up for a matchmaking service like Eden? Why not just choose someone? Shoot, he could have his pick of women, and I doubt many would say no.

But a man with a psychotic stalker who thinks she already owns him? That's enough of a dealbreaker to send most women running.

The nausea eases, but in its place, exhaustion crashes over me like a wave. "Well, why haven't you done anything about it?"

Henry exhales sharply, shaking his head. "Because the police think it's funny. They don't understand how having a woman chase after you the way she does can be dangerous. To them, it's flattering. It's a joke. Besides, technically, she hasn't done anything illegal."

"Nothing illegal? She's *stalking* you, Henry. That is illegal. Haven't you ever filed for a restraining order?"

He lets out a humorless laugh. "You think restraining orders actually work from man to woman? The legal system is gender-biased. If I were stalking her, sure, they'd care. But a woman stalking a man?" His expression darkens, a bitter edge to his voice. "No one cares."

I shake my head, pressing my forehead against his chest. "Why didn't Dexter tell me anything about this? I feel like this is something Eden should've made sure I knew."

Henry cups my face, tilting it up so I have to look at him. He looks miserable, tortured. A wave of pity crashes over me. I can't even begin to imagine what it's been like for him—living with someone like her haunting the edges of his life.

"If you'd known," he asks quietly, "would you have done anything differently?"

Something about the way he says it hurts. There's vulnerability in his voice, a rawness that makes my throat tighten.

I think back to when James left me shattered on the curb, my heart broken into pieces I didn't know how to put back together. I remember how desperately I had wanted this, craved this—the kind of love that could hold me, steady me, make me feel *safe*.

Nobody's perfect. Not even Henry, I realize now.

We all come with our own baggage, our own wounds. And for one reason or another, we were both willing to walk into marriage with a stranger, hoping it would be enough.

And I know, without a doubt, that if I had been shown this man standing before me—*this* man, even with the knowledge that a psychotic stalker was trying to claw her way into our marriage—I still would have chosen him.

I would have married him.

Because I love him.

And in this moment, under the rushing water, as vulnerable as either of us has ever been, that love doesn't just hold steady. It grows.

I press my palm against his chest, feeling the steady thrum of his heart beneath my fingertips, and I shake my head.

His breath shudders as he pulls me closer, his hand pressing firmly against the small of my back, and then he kisses me.

But this kiss is different.

Where the others have been full of passion and desire, a frantic need to *know* each other, *explore* each other—this one is filled with something else entirely.

Sadness.

Forgiveness.

Vulnerability.

Love.

It's the best kiss we've ever had.

So good that when he pulls away, we both sigh.

"What are we going to do?" I whisper.

Henry lets out a laugh—low, almost bitter. He shakes his head. "I have no clue."

"We could always just kill her."

He freezes.

I tilt my head up, watching his expression from beneath my soaked hair.

"I'm joking," I say, rolling my eyes. "Relax. As much as I'd love to take her out to the ocean and feed her to the sharks, I have no desire to spend my life behind bars."

His breath releases, and before I know it, his arms are wrapping around me again.

The water begins to cool, but soon, warmth sparks between us. My fingers trace lightly over his arms, and when he glances down at me, his smile sends butterflies fluttering wildly through my stomach.

Henry kisses me again, slower this time, like he's savoring every second, like the weight of everything— Genevieve, the lies, the past—can't touch us in this moment.

I let myself melt into it. Into *him*. Into the warmth of his touch and the solid strength of his body pressing against mine. Because whatever happens next, whatever nightmare Genevieve still has planned, none of it changes the fact that *he is mine*.

Not hers.

Not ever.

The water grows colder, but neither of us move. His fingers skim my back, and I close my eyes, letting my forehead rest against his. We stay like that, caught in the quiet.

Then Henry exhales, breaking the silence.

"We'll figure it out," he murmurs. "We have to."

We have to.

Because Genevieve isn't going away. She isn't the kind of problem that just... disappears.

I tilt my chin up, studying the face of the man who belongs to *me*—the man I married, the man I love. The man she wants to take from me.

No.

That's not going to happen.

I slide my hands down his chest, feeling the steady, strong beat of his heart beneath my palms. He watches me, his eyes searching, soft and trusting. He still thinks we're in this together. That we'll talk through it and come up with some ideas, wait for the right moment.

But I'm tired of waiting.

I let out a slow, measured breath and pull away, reaching for a towel. "We should get out before we freeze."

Henry nods, but as I step out of the shower, I catch my reflection in the mirror. My soaked hair clings to my shoulders, my lips swollen from his kisses, my eyes dark with something new. I smirk at my reflection and slowly slide my ring back on, twisting it into place.

I meant what I said before.

I have no desire to live my life behind bars.

But I also have no intention of losing my husband.

And if Genevieve won't back off willingly?

Well.

There's more than one way to get rid of a problem.

TWENTY-THREE
HENRY

I need a cigarette.

TWENTY-FOUR

MORGAN

"One passionfruit mocktail."

Luka glances up, a cleaning cloth in one hand, a cup in the other. He catches the edge in my voice, his movements slowing as he takes me in. His gaze flicks around, checking if I'm alone.

I am.

I made sure of it. I waited until the bar was empty, until there were no other staff members hovering nearby, until it was just *us*.

"You sure you don't want strawberry?" he asks casually. "They're just as good."

"Fine. Sure. Whatever." I fold my arms on the bar. "How come you didn't tell me?"

He stiffens. "Tell you what?"

My face twists. "And how did you even *know*?"

Luka exhales through his nose, setting the cup down with a quiet clink. "This is about what Genevieve said, isn't it?"

I don't answer right away. My fingers trace the deep

groove marks she left in the wood, following the scratches almost absentmindedly. "You knew she wasn't what she seemed. You even *warned* me. Which leaves me wondering—how much of our personal lives do all of you staff members know?"

Luka doesn't respond. Instead, he turns away, quietly mixing the strawberry mocktail. He works quickly, efficiently, and within seconds, he slides the glass in front of me.

I lift it, holding the straw to my lips, taking a slow sip.

To my surprise, it is just as good as the passionfruit one. I'm not normally someone who enjoys strawberry-flavored things, but this? It's light, sweet, a little tart.

"It's pretty good," I murmur.

"Told you."

I point at him, my expression unreadable. "Don't try to distract me. You *betrayed* me."

Luka blinks, his expression tightening. "What? How did I betray you?"

"We're supposed to be friends—"

"We are?"

"—and friends are supposed to let each other know that, *hey*, maybe this crazy psycho woman on the resort actually thinks she's married to your husband."

His face darkens, but before he can get a word in, I hold up a hand.

"Now," I say smoothly, "because you make the *best* mocktails, I've decided to forgive you. But you can make it up to me by telling me which suite she's staying in... and giving me the key code to her room."

His jaw drops, then he lets out a disbelieving laugh. "Are you trying to ruin my life?"

"Make it up to me, Luka."

"Do you even know what would happen to me if Eden found out?"

I take a slow sip of my drink. "Make it up to me."

"No. Absolutely not. I'm not doing that."

I sigh dramatically. "Okay, so I guess I'll just have to find out where she's staying myself. And break in. Maybe some shattered glass, maybe a trashed room—who knows what else will happen. Maybe she's sleeping while I do it. Bad things could happen."

His expression hardens. "Don't do that."

I smile.

"I'm serious," he snaps. "Don't."

"Or," I counter smoothly, "you could help me. We wait until she and Brody leave, then we sneak in, I do what I need to do, and we're gone. That way, you don't create more work for one of your fellow... whatever-you-call-your-colleagues." I take another sip of the mocktail and hum. "Really, this is good."

Luka exhales sharply through his nose, visibly struggling to keep his composure.

"Look," I continue, setting my drink down, "either way, I'm breaking into her place. I have to."

He scrubs a hand down his face, lets out another sigh. "What exactly are you trying to do?"

"Honestly?" I lean forward slightly. "I'm just trying to figure this out. I already tried to contact my Eden representative to get me and Henry off this island, but apparently, he's not here. And I'm stuck until he's back, which could be another couple of days." I shake my head. "I don't have that long. Every day that passes, things get worse. So... I want her off the island. And I'm sure there's something in her suite that breaks policy. Some contraband, something we can use to *get rid of her*."

Luka hesitates, then glances over his shoulder, checking the bar. His fingers tighten around the cloth before he slowly sets it down. Then he leans in, lowering his voice.

"Look," he murmurs, "you're going about this all wrong."

I tilt my head, watching him carefully.

He doesn't elaborate. Instead, he shifts slightly, like he's debating whether to continue. The flickering candlelight of the bar casts shadows across his face, highlighting the tension there.

I set my drink down. "Oh? Then tell me—what's the *right* way?"

Luka shakes his head. "You don't want to do this."

"Actually, I do."

"No," he says, quieter this time. "You *don't*."

There's something about the way he says it— controlled, careful, like each word has been measured before leaving his mouth.

I narrow my eyes. "You think I should just leave."

His jaw ticks, but he doesn't respond.

I laugh under my breath, but there's no humor in it. "You're saying I should forget Henry, forget her, and just... go?"

Luka picks up the rag again, gripping it tight enough that I see his knuckles go white.

"Is that what you'd do?" I press. "Run?"

"I'd survive," he says, and that single sentence hits harder than I expect.

I inhale, holding his gaze. "Well, I'm not leaving my husband. That's not a question, that's not up for debate. So if you're trying to push me in that direction, save your breath. I am getting rid of her, and you are helping me."

He stares at me for a long moment, expression unreadable.

I lean in, my voice dropping to a whisper. "Because if you don't... something bad could happen to *me*, too. Would you want that on your conscience?"

His entire body stiffens.

Silence stretches between us, thick with unspoken things. His eyes flick toward the empty space behind me, as if expecting someone to be watching.

I don't move. I don't look away.

Finally, he releases a slow breath, rubbing a hand over his face before muttering, "You're just as insane as she is."

"Maybe." I shrug. "But I'm not wrong."

Luka mutters something under his breath in another language, shaking his head. I can tell he's still trying to convince himself that this is a bad idea—that he shouldn't be involved, that it's not his problem.

But then, he sighs. Deep. Resigned.

And I know I've won.

He grabs a notepad from under the bar and jots something down. It's quick, just a few letters and numbers, and then he tears the page, sliding it toward me.

Her suite number, and the key code that will get me into it.

I tuck it into my palm, smiling. "See? That wasn't so hard."

Luka scowls. "This is the only time I help you. After this, you and I? We don't talk again. Ever."

So he wasn't going to help me figure out when Genevieve and Brody left their suite. That was okay. I figured that was pushing it, anyway.

I grin, lifting my drink. "Not even for another mocktail?"

He doesn't answer. He just picks up the rag again and starts wiping down the counter, like this conversation never happened.

Something about it makes me pause.

But I make to leave, and he says, "She has a spa appointment tomorrow at eleven, Mrs. Langford."

I stop, looking back at him.

Then I smile. "Call me Morgan."

Luka hesitates. It's subtle, but I catch it—the way his fingers twitch, the way his throat bobs like he wants to say something but doesn't.

He only nods.

I walk away, the note burning in my palm, my next move already forming.

TWENTY-FIVE
MORGAN

I linger on the shore after breakfast, the sun already high enough to scatter diamond flecks across the water's surface. Henry's still sifting through shells near the tide line, utterly fascinated by a few he's found. It's oddly endearing.

But I can't focus on him. I can't focus on anything. Not with the clock ticking closer to eleven. Soon enough, I'll be breaking into Suite 8—Genevieve's room.

My skin is clammy, my heart pounding. I try to steady my breathing, but the anxiety is relentless, clawing up my throat.

What if Genevieve comes back early and catches me?

What if Brody is still in the room?

I feel like I'm going to be sick.

All the bravado I had yesterday with Luka has completely evaporated. And the worst part? I can't even tell Henry. He'd lose his mind if he knew I was breaking into the room where his stalker was sleeping. But it has to be done. I have to find something—anything—that will get her off this island.

I check my wristwatch. Fifteen minutes until eleven. Close enough.

All the bravado I had yesterday with Luka has completely evaporated. He tosses aside the duller shells and jogs over, grinning.

"Look at this," he says, holding up a seashell that glimmers like an opal. I understand now why he was so fascinated. It's beautiful, a rare little treasure buried in the sand.

I manage a smile. "That's really pretty."

His grin fades, replaced by a slight frown. "Are you okay? You look kind of... off."

"Yeah, I just—I'm not feeling great."

His brow furrows. "What's wrong?"

"I think I just need to rest," I say, carefully injecting just the right amount of weariness into my voice. My stomach twists with guilt, but this is necessary. "You should stay, though. Keep enjoying the beach. I'll just head up to the room for a bit."

He hesitates, glancing at the water, clearly torn. I know he wants to stay. I'm counting on that.

After a moment, he sighs. "I'll come with you."

I shake my head, getting to my feet and stepping closer, pressing a quick kiss to his cheek.

"No, really, I'll be fine. It's just a headache." I sigh for emphasis, then force a small chuckle. "Besides, you'll just hover and make it worse."

"Excuse me?" He grins, but there's a flicker of concern in his eyes. I watch it shift into reluctant acceptance as I keep smiling, feigning confidence, feigning nonchalance.

"I mean it, Henry. I'll ring the staff if I need anything. Promise."

He exhales through his nose, then nods. "All right, if you insist. But I'm checking on you in an hour."

"Deal."

I turn and walk away, resisting the urge to look back. Because if I do, I'll see him standing there, arms crossed, watching me. And if I see that, the guilt will hit. If the guilt hits, I might lose my nerve.

That can't happen.

So I keep going, stepping off the beach onto the manicured pathways leading to the row of suites. My pulse thrums in my ears, my hands already slick with sweat.

It's surreal, really. As the girl who actively avoided confrontation growing up, I can hardly believe I'm about to break into someone's room.

Even the palm fronds above seem to shudder, like they can sense the pounding of my heart, like they know I'm about to do something reckless.

I pass a few couples and nod at a staff member pushing a cart of fresh linens, forcing myself to move casually, to look normal. But with every step closer to Suite 8, the edge of my nerves sharpens.

And then, there it is.

Suite 8.

I check my watch again. Five past eleven. The suite should be empty now. My hand trembles as I test the handle. Locked. Of course. I swallow hard, reach into my pocket, and pull out the paper Luka gave me. My fingers are shaking as I punch in the key code.

A small green light flashes. A soft click.

Time slows as I push open the door.

A wave of rose and musk-scented air washes over me. But something sharp and cloying lingers beneath it, making my nose crinkle.

I ignore it. Step inside. Shut the door behind me.

Drawing a deep breath, I turn.

The living area is pristine. A sleek glass coffee table holds a neat stack of glossy magazines. A modern sofa faces an enormous window overlooking the ocean, the infinity pool shimmering just beyond.

The only hint of life? An unzipped suitcase in the corner.

I exhale, my pulse slowing just slightly as I repeat the words in my head like a mantra: She's not here.

I move to the bedroom. It's nearly identical to ours—just slightly smaller. The bed is meticulously made, the corners tucked in with almost obsessive precision. A vanity drawer holds an array of products: an elegant brush, expensive skincare brands I don't recognize, a few delicate pieces of jewelry.

I move quietly, methodically, opening drawers, scanning for anything that might prove Genevieve is dangerous. Drugs, maybe. A weapon. Anything.

It's desperate, I know. A flimsy hope. But what else can I do when a stalker is obsessed with my husband?

Something else strikes me as odd. I don't see much of Brody's stuff. Maybe he just doesn't have a lot. I've met men like that before—simple, minimalistic, the kind who travel light.

Genevieve, on the other hand, has enough products to stock a boutique. And her perfume.

God.

It's like she bathed in it. The scent is so overpowering it makes it hard to breathe.

Why does she spray *so* much?

I shake my head as I shut the last drawer, disappointment curling in my chest. I suppose it was too much to hope that whatever contraband she had would be sitting here, out in the open.

But I haven't checked everywhere yet.

Sunlight filters through the half-open window as I move toward the bathroom.

Then I freeze.

My heart seizes, and I stumble back into the bedroom, pressing myself against the wall. Adrenaline surges, sharp and punishing, setting my hands trembling.

Brody is still here.

I saw him—a quick flash of skin and hair in the bathtub. It couldn't have been Genevieve. She doesn't have hair. But I don't think he saw me.

I could still leave.

I start to creep toward the door, but something makes me pause.

That smell...

Slowly, carefully, I inch back to the bathroom entrance and steal a glance inside.

It is Brody in the tub.

But it's all wrong. So, *so* wrong.

My pulse slows, thick with dread. A deeper, heavier ache spreads through me.

He's fully submerged. Dumbbells—the kind from the resort gym—are stacked on his chest, pinning him beneath the water.

Oh God. Brody.

A strangled sound slips from my throat. His eyes are half-open but empty, his lips parted, unmoving. The water is unnervingly still—no bubbles, no ripples, nothing to suggest life.

My gaze drops again to the weights pressing him down.

I stagger back.

I need to run. Need to call for help. My mind spins, tangled in confusion, fear, and disbelief. The world tilts, surreal, like I've stumbled into a nightmare.

Genevieve did this.

I know it in my bones.

Panic crashes through me, drowning out everything but the loudest command in my mind: Get out. Now.

I wrench open the door, not bothering to close it. It slams against the wall, swinging wide, leaving the suite gaping behind me as I tear outside.

But even in the glaring sun, the world still feels dark.

Brody's lifeless eyes are burned into my mind, and Genevieve's rose-and-musk perfume clings to my skin, choking me. My pulse roars in my ears, each step fueled by panic.

I need Luka.

He'll help me report this. Help me get that murderer off the island—lock her away where she belongs.

I sprint past sun-drenched couples, nearly crashing into the bar, my breath ragged.

"Luka!"

He's not alone. His manager stands nearby—the same man who replaced him before. His gaze flicks between us, curious about our familiarity.

Luka's lips press into a thin line, clearly irritated that I'm calling for him so urgently in front of his boss.

"Mrs. Langford, how can I—"

"You have to come. Now."

Concern etches into his face, but the manager steps forward instead.

"Mrs. Langford, is something the matter?"

I can barely force out the words. My voice hitches. "Brody. H-he's dead. In Genevieve's suite. There are—weights on him."

They exchange uncertain glances, not fully grasping what I'm saying.

"He's been murdered!"

Luka looks to his manager. The older man steps in, gripping my shoulder, anchoring me.

"Do not worry, ma'am. I'm sure there's a misunderstanding."

"Misunderstanding?" I stare at him, incredulous. "The man is dead in the bathtub." I turn to Luka, pleading. "Tell him. Tell him how awful Genevieve is, how—"

The man raises a hand, cutting me off with a patronizing smile. "We'll go check it out, okay? But for now, just breathe, Mrs. Langford."

I nod, though my breath still comes in ragged bursts.

"Stay here," he instructs Luka before turning back to me. "I'll be with you momentarily."

Luka pales but nods.

"You need to call the police," I insist, my voice low and desperate. "Get her off this island. Lock her up."

The manager's smile doesn't waver, patronizing as ever. "We will. But let's see what's happening first."

I want to scream at the insanity of walking up there without backup. But part of me needs to see. Needs the confirmation that I'm not losing my mind.

Nearby, couples whisper, casting uneasy glances. I know it bothers the manager, but I'm too shaken to care.

He leads the way, setting a brisk pace that forces me to half-jog to keep up.

Then—

A piercing scream tears through the air.

High, shrill, raw with terror. A sound that sends a wave of cold horror down my spine.

The manager curses and charges forward.

The suite's doors stand wide open, swinging just as I left them. My breath stalls as I follow him inside.

My gaze snaps to the bathroom.

Genevieve stands in front of it, hair disheveled, a pale silk blouse unbuttoned at the collar. Her hands are pressed to her mouth, her expression the picture of perfect horror.

She sees us and gasps, a trembling, helpless sound. Her hands flail toward the bathroom, as if words have failed her.

"Oh my God, there's—he's—" Her voice breaks, choking on the weight of it.

My eyes snap to the tub.

Brody's body is still there. But the dumbbells—the ones that held him under—are gone.

The water, still tinged with soap, laps at his neck. He's unmistakably dead. But the evidence that he was *forced* beneath the surface? Vanished.

I stare, my mouth dry, heart hammering.

Genevieve clings to the doorframe like a grief-stricken widow, her eyes glossy with tears. She looks at us, her expression crumbling.

"M-my... my *husband!*" she wails, her voice breaking.

The manager rushes forward, glancing at the tub. His face hardens as he sees Brody's lifeless form. But instead of alarm, his focus shifts—to comforting her.

Genevieve sobs, shaking. "I found him like this. How —what happened?"

"It's okay, Mrs. Summerson."

She wails again, collapsing to her knees, half-dragging him down with her. "I'm not a Summerson anymore. Brody is dead!"

The manager soothes her, murmuring reassurances.

I stand frozen, fists clenched, rage and disbelief curdling inside me.

She's playing the part perfectly—the devastated, innocent wife who just discovered her husband's body.

But I know what I saw.

I know those weights were there. I saw them. Someone held Brody under, forced the air from his lungs. And that perfume—the sweet, cloying mix of rose and musk—wasn't just a signature scent. It was a mask, meant to cover whatever smell would come from his decaying body. An overwhelming urge surges through me—to scream, to accuse—but the words wedge in my throat.

Because how do I prove she moved the weights? That she's lying?

No one else saw them. And now, she's giving a performance worthy of an Oscar.

"Brody, oh, Brody!" she sobs, turning her face away from the tub in a perfect display of grief. "Why would he... this is just..."

Her voice falls off in supposed grief.

I want to cross the room and shake her, force the truth from her lips. But I can't move. The weight of it, of how neatly she's manipulated the situation, crushes me.

In one swift move, she's erased every trace of evidence that this was her murder.

The manager helps her to her feet, murmuring reassurances as he leads her past me. His focus is on her, on the grieving widow she's pretending to be. But when he looks back at the bathroom, he misses how she looks up at me—and winks.

My breath catches.

You monster.

"Don't touch anything," the manager warns me, his tone firm. "Come with us."

I want to stay. To fight. To tell him she did it, and tear the room apart until I find those weights and shove them in his face.

But somehow, I know the truth.

I wouldn't find them.

She's gotten away with murder.

TWENTY-SIX

MORGAN

A mandatory counseling session.

An innocent man had been murdered at the resort, and apparently, that was all I needed. A little therapy. A few deep breaths. Truth be told, I wanted to take Henry and run. Find the fastest way off this cursed island. I would have swam if I had to.

But Henry convinced me to stay. Said we'd get through the session, speak to our Eden representative, and figure things out. I only agreed because of one thing.

Dexter was back.

The staff let it slip, and suddenly, I had a reason to sit through this charade. It seemed all it took to get him urgently back on site was a dead body.

I close my eyes. I can still see Brody floating in the water, his lifeless, fogged-over eyes staring at nothing. It haunted me all night, made sleep impossible. Still haunts me now. But not as much as the woman who killed him.

If she was willing to murder him—a man who was kind, if a little overly so, who probably just wanted her to love him as he loved her—then what was stopping her from coming for me next? She'd already proven she would do anything to clear a path to Henry.

I never thought murder would be on that list.

A warm hand closes over mine. Henry. I turn, expecting a smile, some attempt to reassure me. There isn't one. His gaze is fixed on the blank wall, troubled.

A wave of pity washes over me. I imagine he never saw this coming—never thought his stalker would be capable of this. It must be disturbing for him, knowing what this means for the future.

Pack the bags. Leave the businesses, the friends, the family behind. Sell the house. Start over, all in the vain hope that we could be safe.

I lean my head back and let out an explosive sigh. It finally draws Henry's attention. His lips part, like he wants to say something, to soothe me. But before he can, the door to the counseling room swings open.

Dr. Warren appears. "Mr. and Mrs. Langford. Please come in." She doesn't wait for us, just turns and disappears inside.

I stay put. This island, and that counseling room, is the last place I want to be.

Henry knows it too. Knows I hate these counseling sessions just as much as he does. Funny. The only reason it's here is to help our marriage out in these early stages, and instead, it seemed like Dr. Warren's interference has done the opposite. It feels like it's hindering us, keeping us tethered to the ground instead of letting us fly.

Well, that's not entirely true. What's keeping us tethered to the ground is the undeniable weight of that awful cow, Genevieve.

"Henry."

A voice, warm and languid, shocks me back into focus. I jolt up out of my chair and step inside.

Three chairs, not two. And in the far-left seat, sitting like she belongs, is Genevieve.

Henry exhales, staring at her with what looks like... sadness?

"Eve... I—"

I cut through the moment before he can say anything else.

"What is she doing here?" My voice is sharp, slicing through the air.

Dr. Warren's expression doesn't flicker. "Please sit down, Morgan."

I don't move. "I asked you a question. What is she doing here?"

My knuckles turn white, fear and fury twisting through me. The scent of rose and musk wafts through the air, suffocating me and dragging back to the bathroom of her suite, back to the dead man drowning. As much as I want to face her, I can't even look in her direction.

Dr. Warren gives me a patient, knowing smile and gestures toward the chair, as if she doesn't need to repeat herself.

I glance at Henry, waiting for him to stand with me, to end this nightmare before it begins. Instead, I watch him sink into the middle chair—between Genevieve and the seat meant for me.

My stomach twists.

Why?

He listened to me all night as I told him over and over how I found Brody dead in that bathtub. Not once did he interrupt. Like the perfect husband, he held me, loved me, reassured me in soft whispers, knowing it was the only thing he could do. And now, he's willing to sit next to that monster?

Silence settles over the room like a heavy fog, and the tension pulls taut as a wire, threatening to snap.

Henry exhales, a rough, exhausted sound. He looks at me, his eyes bloodshot, lined with something fragile.

"Morgan," he whispers. A plea. A quiet, desperate beg.

I swallow hard, forcing myself to look at her.

Genevieve sits unnaturally still, her body posed just enough to appear broken, fragile. Her usual polish is gone —hair slightly unkempt, lips trembling. Bloodshot eyes that haven't shed a single tear.

To Henry, to Dr. Warren, she looks devastated. But I see the truth. I see the glint beneath the mask, the savage amusement curling at the edges of her mouth, just enough to dare me to sit or walk away.

I curl my fingers into fists, nails digging into my palms deep enough to cut. I let the pain ground me, and then, slowly, I lower myself into the chair.

Dr. Warren waits a beat before folding her hands neatly in front of her. "Now, as you've noticed, I've invited Genevieve here because I—and the rest of the Eden staff—believe that today, a collective therapy session is necessary. A traumatic loss has—"

"Traumatic loss?" My voice is sharp, cutting through

her words. "Brody was murdered. And she—" I gesture, my finger hovering in Genevieve's direction, "she was the one who murdered him."

Dr. Warren doesn't flinch. Doesn't acknowledge the accusation. She gives me that same patronizing smile.

"Please don't interrupt me, Morgan. There will be time for all of us to speak." A pause. She tilts her head, and adds, "But as important as it is to speak, it is twice as important to listen."

A scoff slips out before I can stop it. Listen? To this? While a cold-blooded murderer sits just inches from my husband?

I glance at Henry, expecting support.

But what I find instead?

Disappointment.

It settles in his features, a quiet sigh in his expression, a slight downturn of his mouth.

I sit back, arms crossed, pulse thrumming with barely restrained rage. Am I pushing too hard? Am I seeming hysterical, and that's why nobody believes me? I can't understand it. There was a *body*. Shouldn't that be enough evidence for people to question things?

Dr. Warren clears her throat. "As I was saying, Brody —" She glances down at her notes. "—Summerson passed away, and—"

A sharp, broken sob cuts through the air.

We all turn.

Genevieve dabs at her nose with a cloth, eyes screwed shut as if she's barely keeping herself together. Her shoulders tremble. Her lips part in a shuddering breath. Then, as if suddenly aware of our eyes on her, she gathers herself.

She sniffs, clears her throat, and looks at each one of us in turn.

"I'm sorry," she whispers, voice trembling. "I just... does this make me a widow?"

Henry shifts, his face twisted into an awkward expression. Then, his hand moves. A small, hesitant pat to her hand.

I freeze. My stomach plummets.

"I think so," he mutters.

Did he just... reassure her? I'm lost for words.

"This session," Dr. Warren continues, her voice smooth, practiced, completely detached from reality, "is about coming together and repairing relationships. We are not here to discuss the facts of Brody's unfortunate passing, but instead, to discuss our feelings."

Is this some kind of sick joke? Our *feelings*? Is she serious?

"Would any of you like to start?"

I let out a slow breath, pressing my fingers to my temple. Where would I even begin? The disbelief is too thick, too tangled in my throat for me to find words.

Not that I have to.

Genevieve is more than happy to fill the silence.

"Thank you, Dr. Warren." Her voice is soft, measured, carrying the perfect amount of grief. "I'm so glad Eden cares about us so much. But there's just... one thing I'm struggling to understand."

Dr. Warren nods. "Please, share that with us."

Genevieve hesitates, a delicate pause—just long

enough to make it seem authentic. Then, she speaks, "If... if you listen to Morgan's version of events, then it sounds like she broke into my suite. But what I can't understand is why?"

"A valid question. Morgan?"

They all look at me, and one by one, I look back. I scoff, shaking my head. "You didn't murder him? Well, I didn't break in. I wasn't even there."

Genevieve's brow furrows, her confusion carefully measured. She folds her hands in her lap and glances toward Dr. Warren. "But if that's true, then how did you warn the staff so quickly? They arrived just moments after I found him."

My lip curls as I lean forward. "I think your memory's a little messed up. It's okay, it happens. Doesn't trauma do that, Dr. Warren?"

Dr. Warren presses her lips into a thin line, seeing through my attempt. I know it won't hold. The timeline is sitting somewhere in her notes, neatly recorded alongside the bar manager's report.

Before she can correct me, Henry lifts a hand.

"She did break in."

Dr. Warren's eyes widen, and so do mine. I glance at Henry, betrayal hitting fast and sharp.

"I'm sorry, Morgan, but I want our marriage to be built on truth. And let's face it, that hasn't exactly been the case."

My pulse pounds in my ears. "What do you mean?" My voice is low, controlled, but my eyes flicker past him —to Genevieve, smiling at him, like she's falling for him all over again.

I clench my jaw, muscles ticking. "What are you saying, Henry?"

"I'm saying you lied. *Again.*"

"Again?"

"Yes, again. The first time, you told me you weren't meeting Eve at the spa. And you went anyway. You deliberately lied then, just like you lied yesterday when you told me you weren't feeling well. You made that up to sneak off and break into her suite."

I can see the hurt in his eyes, and somehow, I—

Dr. Warren and Genevieve blur into the background. It's just Henry now, sitting across from me. His expression isn't hard or cruel—it's worse. It's a deep disappointment, like he's questioning his choice to keep me as his wife.

A realization settles in my chest, pressing down, making it hard to breathe.

I broke his trust.

I *did* lie. I had told him I wasn't feeling well, knowing I had every intention of sneaking off. I had gone behind his back. I had looked him in the eye and fed him something false, and now I was paying the price for it.

But couldn't he see past that? Couldn't he see that there was something bigger happening here?

"Do you believe me?" My voice is quieter now, more restrained.

He exhales. "Morgan..."

I shake my head. "Not about breaking in. About Genevieve." I meet his gaze, searching for something— anything—that tells me I haven't lost him completely. "Do you believe me?"

He hesitates.

The pause is barely there, just a fraction of a second, but I feel it like a punch to the gut. I watch him wrestle with it, see the part of him that wants to believe me fighting against the part of him that has already started pulling away.

Finally, he sighs. "I don't think she killed Brody."

The floor tilts beneath me. "What?"

"But I don't think you were lying about that either," he says carefully. "As you said a minute ago, trauma distorts our memory, right? Well, maybe you saw things that weren't there."

Something in my chest clenches.

Like the weights weighing him down.

The image of Brody's body flashes through my mind —his lifeless eyes, the subtle bruises on his chest where the weights sat, the eerie stillness of the water.

A wave of nausea rolls through me.

How could he sit there, with everything we know about what a monster Genevieve is, and act as if *I* might be confused?

My voice is shaking now, my control slipping. "Henry... I didn't imagine those weights."

He looks away from me, and I stare at him, my heart twinging with pain. Had I been so focused on Genevieve that I'd been unknowingly rotting my own marriage? Had I played into her game, by lying to him?

"She's playing us," I whisper.

"Not this time."

"She's playing you," I snap. "And you're letting her."

His jaw tightens, but he doesn't immediately respond.

"What if you're wrong?" he finally asks.

"I'm not." I say.

But Henry is already looking away again, jaw set, eyes clouded with doubt.

Dr. Warren clears her throat. "I think we've spent enough time on this." She flips a page in her notes, barely sparing me a glance before continuing, her voice smooth, clinical. "There's another matter I'd like to discuss. In the official report, it's noted that when you discovered Brody's body, you didn't immediately go to your husband." She looks up at me now, raising a brow. "You ran to Luka."

The words drop into the room like a stone.

Henry's head snaps toward me. "Who's Luka?"

My face goes pale.

"Henry," I say quickly, but my voice is thin, unsteady.

His eyes darken, his posture stiffening as he waits. "Who. Is. Luka?"

"I—" My throat closes. I feel Genevieve's gaze on me, feel Dr. Warren watching, analyzing, waiting for my response, but it's Henry that makes my pulse spike. There's something different about his expression now. It's not just disappointment. Not just doubt.

It's anger.

He's never looked at me like this before.

I force myself to swallow, but it doesn't help. "Luka is —he's a staff member."

"A staff member?" His voice is sharp now, cutting

through the air. "And you know him so well that you ran to him? Over me?"

I shake my head. "It wasn't like that."

"Then explain it."

I open my mouth, but the words won't come. How could I explain something I hadn't even thought about before this moment? The instinct that had driven me? The way my feet had moved, my mind made up before I even had time to process it?

Henry waits, his jaw clenched.

Genevieve shifts in her seat, watching with a sly grin that she's fighting to keep from spreading across her face, while Dr. Warren tilts her head, staring at me with that cold, neutral expression.

And suddenly, the weight of all of it crashes into me.

With them all standing against me, I have never felt lonelier in my life.

"I don't—" I start, but it comes out shaky, barely above a whisper. "I don't know."

Henry exhales, a sharp, disbelieving sound. "You don't know?"

I force myself to meet his eyes, even though I can barely stand to see what's in them. "I didn't think. I just— Luka was there. He was working. I trusted him. I—" I break off, shaking my head, scrambling, trying to find the words that will fix this.

"But you didn't trust me," Henry finishes.

I flinch. "It wasn't about that."

"Then what was it about?"

"It was about getting her off the resort!" The words burst out of me, raw and too loud in the suffocating quiet of the room. "I wasn't thinking—I just—I just needed help, and I thought of Luka, because he *works* here."

"That's not good enough." His voice is low now, controlled, but I feel the rage in it.

My heart slams against my ribs. "Henry—"

"I'm your husband." His voice is steady, but the anger is right there, simmering just beneath the surface. "And when you were in trouble—when you found a body—you didn't come to me. You went to some random staff member."

"He's not random." The words slip out before I can stop them.

A sharp silence settles over the room.

Henry leans back slightly, exhaling through his nose like he's trying to control himself. "No?" He nods slowly. "So what is he, then?"

I shake my head, feeling the walls closing in.

"It's not like that," I whisper.

But even I don't sound convinced.

Henry lets out a slow breath, his hands gripping the arms of his chair. His expression has shifted into something unreadable, but I know what's coming before he even speaks.

"I'm done." His voice is flat, final.

A sick feeling washes over me. "Henry—"

He pushes back from the table, the chair scraping against the floor as he stands. He doesn't look at me, doesn't hesitate, just moves for the door.

"Henry, please." I reach for him, my voice quiet, unsteady, but he keeps walking.

He doesn't stop.

Doesn't even turn around.

The door swings shut behind him, the sound slamming through the room like a warning shot.

I sit there, my fingers curled into fists against my chest, barely able to breathe.

Dr. Warren exhales, closing her folder with the same calm efficiency she's maintained this entire time. "I think that's enough for today." She stands, smoothing out her blouse, already distancing herself from whatever just unraveled in this room. "We can try again at another time."

I stare at her, wanting to argue, to make her see how wrong this all is, but she's already heading for the door. I watch as she disappears through it without another glance in my direction, leaving me alone with Genevieve.

The silence stretches, thick and suffocating.

For a moment, she stays perfectly still, her hands folded in her lap, the picture of quiet devastation. Then she exhales, slow and satisfied, and when she lifts her head, the mask is gone.

Her lips pull into a soft, knowing smile.

"Well," she murmurs, shifting slightly in her seat. "That was something, wasn't it?"

My body is stiff, my pulse hammering against my ribs, but I refuse to look away. "You don't get to win."

Genevieve lets out a small, amused hum, tilting her head as if I've said something funny. "Win?" She leans forward, her gaze flickering over me, evaluating, dissecting. "Morgan, you don't even know what game you're playing."

My jaw tightens. "Henry doesn't belong to you."

She lifts a brow, her smile deepening. "That's where you're wrong. Henry doesn't belong to *you*."

I shake my head, my throat tight. "There's something wrong with you. *Actually* wrong."

Genevieve gives a small, thoughtful nod, as if she's considering it, as if she's genuinely mulling over my words, but then she lets out a soft laugh. "You keep telling yourself that."

A cold weight settles in my chest, pressing down, making it hard to breathe. There's a certainty in her tone that terrifies me, a finality that makes me feel like I've already lost.

She stands with a sigh, stretching her arms like she's shaking off the last remnants of whatever performance she put on in this room. "I should go check on him. He must be so upset." She takes a few steps toward the door, then pauses, looking back at me. "Try to get some rest, Morgan. You look exhausted."

And then she's gone.

I sit there, frozen, staring at the empty space where she stood, feeling my world close in on itself. For the first time, I start to wonder if I'm ever going to get off this island.

TWENTY-SEVEN
MORGAN

I'm still reeling from the aftermath of the counseling session as I step outside alone. I have no idea where Henry went or if Genevieve actually caught up with him. But right now, I can't bring myself to care. I'm too numb for that.

With slow, aimless steps, I move along the path, passing happy couples who have no idea how good they have it—free of stalkers, obsessives, manipulative monsters who would kill to have their hands on their happiness.

The world around me is blissful, perfect. The ocean stretches endlessly under a wide, cloudless sky. The manicured resort glows beneath it, framed by swaying palm trees. Laughter rings in the distance, echoing in my head like a cruel reminder of everything being taken from me.

Instinct pulls me toward it. Some unconscious part of me wants to be near that warmth, as if proximity to happiness might be enough to absorb even a sliver of it.

Before I even realize it, I'm back at the courtyard pool, surrounded by smiling faces.

I hate them all.

My eyes drift to the bar, and I see a man with his back turned, washing glasses.

Luka.

Relief flutters through me. I slide onto a barstool, pressing my hands to the smooth surface, resting my forehead against it. My fingers trace the faint grooves in the wood—marks Genevieve left behind. I wonder how hard she must have scratched, how much it must have hurt, for her nails to carve into something so solid.

"One passionfruit mocktail," I say quietly.

He doesn't respond. He keeps his back to me, wiping down another glass.

I sigh, shaking my head. "You're mad at me too?" My voice is tired, resigned. "Look, I'm sorry. I didn't mean to drag you into all of this. I just... I thought you could help."

The man turns.

And it's not Luka.

From behind, the resemblance was nearly perfect, but the face is wrong—too unfamiliar, too jarring. This man's mustache is thick and out of place, his brows too heavy.

"Help?" His accent is thicker than Luka's. "I would be glad to do so. How may I assist?"

I frown, the disorientation still settling in. "Where's Luka?"

The man's expression flickers with brief confusion, but a moment later, understanding dawns. "Ah, I had heard a Mrs. Langford would be asking after him. You must be she."

I blink, forcing myself to be patient. He's just a staff member. He's not part of this, not part of any of my problems, and doesn't deserve to be on the receiving end of my frustration. I remind myself to stay calm.

But he doesn't add anything else.

I exhale, feeling my temper fray. "Just call me Morgan. Where's Luka?"

His smile dims slightly, and something in his gaze shifts—just enough to make my stomach tighten. "My apologies, Mrs. Langford, but Luka's services are no longer available."

I straighten. "What?"

"His services are no longer available."

"Yeah, I heard you." I keep my voice even, though a pulse of unease skates down my spine. "But why?"

He hesitates, then shakes his head. "Unfortunately, I cannot comment on the dismissal of another employee, or his removal from the island. However, if you truly wish to know, you may contact your Eden representative. They should be able to answer your inquiry."

I stare at him. "But you're literally working his shift."

"Yes, ma'am, I am." He smiles again, as if that explains everything.

A quiet stretch of silence passes between us. His expression never wavers.

"Fine. You want to help me?" I ask, folding my arms against the bar. "Get me my Eden representative. Dexter. He's supposed to be back on the island."

The man dips his head. "Of course, Mrs. Langford. I will call him."

"No. I want him here."

The bartender hesitates for the briefest second, but he doesn't argue. He sets down the glass and cloth, walks to the phone, and dials a number. I watch as he listens, nodding along with whatever response he's given before setting the receiver back down.

"Dexter will be on his way shortly." His polite, detached tone hasn't changed. "May I prepare a drink for you while you wait?"

I study him, something cold settling in my stomach. He speaks like a lifeless bot, like nothing happening here is the least bit unusual.

I miss Luka. At least he had some life in him.

I lean back against the bar. "Let's try your passion-fruit mocktail."

A few minutes later, he slides the drink across the counter, clearly pleased with himself. I take a sip as he turns away.

It's nowhere near as good as Luka's.

I set the glass down, barely suppressing a grimace. Too sweet. Too artificial. It doesn't have the sharp citrus bite that Luka's did, the balance of tart and sweet that made it worth drinking. This is just syrup and ice, drowning in a cheap imitation of something that was once good.

Just like everything else on this island.

I push it away and rest my elbows on the bar, rubbing my temples. My head throbs, whether from exhaustion or the weight of everything pressing down on me, I don't know. The new bartender moves in my periphery, methodically cleaning, acting like none of this is unusual —like I'm not sitting here, barely holding myself together.

Luka is gone.

It's not like he got sick or decided to quit. He was removed. And that realization creeps over my skin like a cold sweat. Because of *me*.

I don't know how much time passes before I hear approaching footsteps. Slow, steady, unhurried.

I don't lift my head. I don't need to.

Dexter slides onto the barstool beside me, unbuttons the top button of his blazer, and sets his hands on the counter with a casual ease that makes my stomach churn. He must know I'm unraveling at the seams.

He tips his head slightly in my direction. "How are you, Morgan?"

His voice is smooth, almost kind. But that's the thing about Dexter, isn't it? Everything he says is too measured, his tone too perfect, all designed to put people at ease. It doesn't work on me. Not anymore.

I stare at my untouched drink, fingers curling against the bar top.

I could laugh. I could scream. I could tell him exactly how I'm doing, how I had felt *so* happy only for it all to be stolen from me on the grounds of a manipulative liar. I could tell him just how badly I want to walk into Genevieve's suite and wrap my hands around her throat. But I don't think that'd end well for me.

Instead, I swallow the lump in my throat and say the only thing I can manage.

"I want us off this island."

I finally turn to him, searching his face for something —anything—that will tell me whether he's here to help me or here to manage me.

Dexter only smiles.

"I can understand your stress. You just underwent a traumatic experience, and from what Dr. Warren tells me, are struggling with your marriage."

Of course, he'd spoken to Dr. Warren. Dexter was nothing if not thorough. He'd want every detail, every angle, before stepping into a situation.

I rake my hands through my hair, releasing it with an exasperated sigh. "That's not even remotely true. I'm not struggling with my marriage. I'm struggling with her. Genevieve. She's interfering, causing problems where there shouldn't even be any."

Dexter watches me, his expression unreadable. When he finally speaks, his voice is calm. Too calm. "Possessiveness and jealousy are normal feelings, you know. It is perfectly acceptable for you to have them."

The words send a sharp jolt of fury through me.

I slam my fist against the bar. The sudden thud makes the bartender jump, his hand slipping on a glass. Dexter's eyes flicker toward the movement, his mouth pulling into the faintest frown.

"I'm not feeling possessive. I'm not feeling jealous." My voice is shaking now, anger rolling under the surface, barely restrained. "All I feel is one thing: the need to get me and Henry off this island. So I need you to arrange transportation."

A beat of silence.

Dexter doesn't blink.

I grit my teeth, my patience gone. "I'm not asking you, Dexter. I'm telling you. Do you understand?"

And then, he smiles.

That same, practiced, infuriating smile. Smooth. Polished. Like I'm being managed.

I clench my fists, wondering if I'll have to strangle him first before I get to Genevieve.

"There is still one crucial part of the Eden process that must be completed before leaving the island," he says.

I blink. My mind stalls for a second, trying to process what I just heard.

"You can't just keep me here." The words come out slow, disbelieving. "It's illegal."

Dexter folds his hands neatly in front of him. "Morgan, did you not read the entire application process?"

I hesitate.

I think I did. But that night... I'd been distraught. Desperate. It's possible I skimmed.

His gaze sharpens, like he already knows the answer. "The final step of the Eden process requires a reaffirmation of vows at the end of your stay, ensuring that when couples leave, they are not only satisfied with our services —but with each other."

I exhale sharply, forcing down my frustration. "Fine. Great. Set it up for me and Henry, so we can get out of here."

"I would be happy to." He nods, like this is some kind of business transaction. "However, as you should know, the island is quite remote. We are only able to facilitate transportation in dire circumstances or when multiple couples are ready to depart."

"This isn't dire?"

Dexter's smile doesn't waver. "A want does not qualify as a need."

I press my hands flat against the bar, taking a slow breath, steadying myself. "Fine. When's the soonest we can do this vow renewal?"

"You and Henry still have five more days to enjoy the resort. Then we'll proceed with the final step."

Five days.

The words sink like a stone in my stomach.

Five more days of Genevieve. Five more days of her cruel manipulations. Five more days of watching her dig a chasm between Henry and me, while I scramble to hold onto him.

"What if there is no final step? Genevieve doesn't have Brody anymore, so shouldn't she be taken off the island?" I ask, knowing it was a pathetic attempt to remove her from our lives.

In response, Dexter raises a brow and says, "Despite her grief, she has graciously expressed willingness to hold out for five days until the next available transpiration."

I'll bet she has.

I tighten my grip against the counter, fingers pressing into the polished wood. "So that's it, then. We can't leave?"

Dexter exhales through his nose, as if I'm being difficult. "Morgan, I assure you, we have structured Eden's process with years of success behind us. The reaffirmation of vows is a necessary conclusion. Every couple who

departs does so feeling completely secure in their relationship."

His words are so controlled that it makes me want to
break something. How many times has he rehearsed this
script? How many couples has he said these exact
words to?

But this isn't just a script. It's a prison sentence. And
I'm not leaving. Not yet.

Dexter watches me process it, his expression cool,
waiting. Like he knows I'll come to terms with it eventually. Like he's seen it happen a thousand times before.

"Take this opportunity to enjoy your time here," he
says, shifting to a softer tone, as if that will make any of
this easier to swallow. "Spend time with Henry. Relax.
Enjoy a drink." He motions to the bartender with a small
nod. "Try the strawberry mocktail. I believe you'll like it
more than the passionfruit."

The bartender nods and starts preparing it, but I
barely register the movement, because my brain is still
stuck on one thing.

If nobody is allowed to leave the island unless they're
part of a group, then that means...

Luka is still here.

The realization slams into me like a rush of ice water.
The barman said that he couldn't comment on the
dismissal or *removal* of another employee from the island.
As Dexter's footsteps fade into the background, the
sounds of the resort twist and warp around me, until all I
can hear is the thundering pulse of my own heartbeat.

Luka didn't leave. He couldn't have.

So where is he?

Five whole days?

The idea of waiting that long, letting Genevieve play her games and destroy my marriage makes me sick. I can't just sit and twiddle my thumbs. I need to figure something out, find answers to either get her off the island or get *us* off the island.

And I have a gut feeling that Luka knows something that can help.

The sun starts dipping toward the horizon, casting nightfall across the resort and draping it all in shadows. I should be headed back to my suite, back to Henry, but I'm not sure I'm ready to face him. Not until I can prove that I wasn't lying.

I'm *not* unstable, no matter what he or Dr. Warren or even Dexter may think.

I keep my head ducked, avoiding the parts of the resort filled with staff and couples living their lives in their paradise. My heart pounds against my ribs, but I force myself to walk with purpose. Looking guilty is the fastest way to get caught.

The only building that I can think of that Luka might be in is the building the counseling sessions are held in. The counseling sessions were only held in one section, but the building was far larger than that. So the question was... what else was there?

The building looms ahead, its windows dark except for a single light. I've never approached the building from this side, so far off the paved path for guests, but it looks far less friendly than the front.

I pause behind a cluster of palm trees, studying the entrance. Not seeing any sign of staff members, I decide to slip through the growing dark and try my hand at the door.

But sure enough, the handle doesn't give.

There's a keycard reader to the side, with a red light striping its top. I bite my lip, knowing that it'd mean I need to get my hands on a staff card. Which means I need to find a staff member.

As if summoned by my thoughts, a shadow moves at the corner of the building. I dart into the nearby bushes, hardly daring to breathe. A maintenance worker rounds the corner, clipboard in hand, completely lost in thought and unaware of my presence.

I wait until he's close enough, then step out.

"Excuse me," I say, making my voice sound small and embarrassed. "I'm so sorry to bother you, but I'm completely turned around. I was looking for the restroom and somehow ended up outside."

He startles, nearly dropping his clipboard. "Ma'am? This area is staff only."

"Is it? I'm sorry, I didn't know." I wrap my arms around myself like I'm cold, vulnerable. "I was at a late counseling session—it ran long—and I got lost on my way out. Could you help me find my way back to the main path?"

His expression softens with concern. "Of course. Follow me."

As he turns to lead the way, I see it—the keycard dangling from a retractable cord on his belt. One swift movement is all it would take. But I can't just grab it. That'd get me in trouble, and to be honest, I'm not sure what Henry would do if he found out what I was trying to do.

Instead, I stumble forward, letting my ankle twist beneath me. I cry out, falling against him.

"Oh!" I gasp, clutching at his arm. "I'm so sorry—my ankle—"

"It's alright," he says, steadying me. "Let me help you."

As he supports me, I let my hand brush against his side, my finger clumsily unclipping the keycard. By the time I straighten, I've got the card in my pocket.

I study his face, looking for some sign that he's noticed. But to my amazement, he didn't. Somehow, I actually *successfully* pickpocketed him.

The thought brings an unbidden smile to my face. "Actually, I think I'm okay. Look, I see the main path now. Thank you so much for your help. I appreciate you. Really, I do."

Before he can respond, I'm already walking away, forcing myself not to run. I don't look back to see whether he's noticed the missing card. I just keep moving, heart hammering in my chest, until I've circled back to the service entrance.

The card works with a soft beep, and the door unlocks. I slip inside, immediately enveloped by the sterile chill of air conditioning. The hallway before me is dimly lit by emergency exit signs, casting everything in an eerie red glow.

I grimace, taking it all in. It's clear this side of the resort isn't meant to cater to the guests' sense of paradise.

As I move through the hallways, I listen for any sound of movement. Carefully, I try doors as I pass them —most are locked, but a few open to reveal ordinary offices. Filing cabinets. Nothing that screams, *We're holding your bartender prisoner.*

Then I reach a door different from the others. Heavier. With a second keycard reader that requires a code as well. The label beside it reads simply: "Restricted."

I press the stolen keycard against the reader. The light flashes red. Of course—this maintenance worker wouldn't have access to restricted areas.

I'm about to turn away when I notice something strange. The door isn't fully closed. There's a tiny gap, barely noticeable unless you're looking for it. As if someone left in a hurry and didn't check that it locked behind them.

I hold my breath and push gently. The door swings open.

The area beyond is nothing like the polished perfection of the resort's public spaces. Exposed pipes run along the ceiling. The walls are bare concrete, the floor utilitarian tile. It feels like I've stepped behind the curtain of a theater, seeing the crude machinery that creates the illusion of magic and paradise.

Goosebumps pass over my skin, but I push onward, following the corridor past doors with small windows. I glimpse through one, and see shelves stocked with supplies for the bar and kitchen. Another has medicinal supplies, along with medication vials and syringes.

I breathe a sigh of relief. This place was just storage for the entire resort. I allow myself a small smile, shaking my head. Can't believe I was letting this place creep me out.

Then I hear a voice—low, frustrated.

"I told you everything. I don't know how much she knows."

Luka.

I duck, my eyes jolting wide, and hurry toward the door at the back of the hallway. Light is spilling through the cracks, and with my heart jumping into my throat, I peer through the gap.

The room beyond is small, clinical. White walls, bright fluorescent lighting. And there, sitting on a narrow cot, is Luka.

He's not tied up. There are no visible restraints. But the door to the small room he's in has no handle on the inside. It's a cell, dressed up to look like a recovery room.

"Are you sure?"

I draw back at the sound of another voice. I can't see

the woman from where I'm crouching, but if she's in there, then that means there's only one way out...

And I'm right by it.

Wincing, I squeeze myself into the opposite corner, so that when the door swung open, it'd at least hide me. It's not the best option, but it's the *only* one. There's nowhere else to hide in this hallway.

"I'm sure. I wouldn't hold anything back from you. Trust me."

A beat passes, then the woman speaks. "Okay, I trust you. Hang tight, we'll be back."

I press my hand over my mouth to still the sound of my breathing just as the door slams open, painfully hitting against my knee. A woman wearing a long white coat strides down the hallway without looking back.

Scrambling, I sneak into the room before she sees me, taking care to leave the card in the crack of the door. The last thing I need is to get stuck in here.

"Luka," I whisper.

His head snaps up, eyes widening in shock. "What are you—you can't be here."

"I *knew* you were still on the island. What happened? Why are they keeping you here?"

He stands, moving to the glass partition that separates us. There's a small speaking grate at mouth level. "You need to leave. Now. If they find you here—"

"I'm not leaving without answers," I cut him off. "What is this place? Why are you locked up?"

Luka presses his palms against the glass, his expression pained. "Because I talked to you. Because I cared.

Because I warned you about Genevieve when I should have stayed quiet."

My stomach drops. "This is because of me?"

"No," he says firmly. "This is because of them. Eden. The whole system they've built here." He glances nervously at the door. "Morgan, I don't have much time. They'll be coming for me soon."

"Coming for you? What does that even mean?"

His eyes meet mine, and I see real fear there. "Listen to me. The answers you're looking for are going to be in your counselor's files, okay? You *need* to get to them."

Ice crawls down my spine. "Dr. Warren? But—"

"Don't bother with your files, or hers. Look for *his*."

"Who?" I ask, pressing my hand against the partitioned glass. It takes me a moment to realize who he's talking about. My mouth parts. "You mean Henry?"

"I told you. Nothing is what it seems."

"But Luka, I—"

"Stop!" He seethes, eyes darting madly toward the door. Footsteps are echoing in the hallway. "There's a hidden cabinet behind his bookshelf. The lever is disguised as a book, okay? 'Paradise Lost.' Now hide!"

I frantically look around for a place to hide.

"Under the desk," Luka hisses. "Now!"

I dive for the metal desk in the corner, folding myself into the knee space just as the door swings open. My keycard clatters to the ground, and a pair of expensive leather loafers pause.

I recognise the crisp crease of dress pants when they crouch down and a hand grabs the card. It's Dexter.

A beat passes, the tension of the moment constricting itself around my neck, squeezing the air from me. My eyes widen, and I carefully push myself backward, like it'd help.

Then he grunts and tucks the card into the pocket of his pants.

"Mr. Novak," Dexter says. "It's time."

"We don't need to do this," Luka responds, his voice steady despite everything. "I'm positive she doesn't know."

"Well, I'm pleased to hear that. I really am," Dexter says, his tone almost gentle. "But unfortunately, you have exposed yourself as a risk to everything we're doing here. So the interrogation is over. Instead, we're at the point of reaching a solution."

Another pair of shoes enters—white sneakers. Medical shoes.

"Hold out your arm, please," a woman's voice instructs.

I hear movement, then Luka's sharp intake of breath. "Wait, please—"

"This won't hurt," the woman says. "Just a small pinch."

I clamp my hand over my mouth to keep from crying out. I want to leap out, to stop them, but what would that accomplish? They'd just restrain me too, and most probably destroy my marriage with Henry. I'd lose everything.

"What is that?" Luka asks, panic edging his voice. "What are you giving me?"

"Something to help you relax," Dexter says calmly. "It's better this way. Painless."

"No," Luka gasps. "Please—"

"The tightness in your chest is normal," the woman adds clinically. "It will pass quickly."

I hear Luka's breathing grow ragged, then a choking sound that makes bile rise in my throat.

"How long until full cardiac arrest?" Dexter asks.

"Thirty seconds. It mimics a natural heart attack. The autopsy will show nothing suspicious."

"Good. Stick the body in the freezer, next to Brody Summerson. Once transport has been arranged, we can return him and the unfortunate news to his family."

I remain frozen in my hiding spot, tears streaming silently down my face, as Luka's desperate gasps for air grow weaker, then stop entirely.

"Time of death, 10:47 PM," the woman states. "I'll note it as a tragic accident in the report."

Their voices fade as they move toward the door. I stay motionless, barely breathing.

"Have security sweep the grounds," Dexter says. "I found a maintenance card on the ground. I want to know where it came from."

"Of course, sir."

I wait until their footsteps have disappeared from view before crawling out from under the desk and sticking my hand in the door just in time to keep it from clicking shut. My limbs go numb, disconnected from my body.

Luka lies motionless on the cot, his eyes open and glassy, staring at nothing. A small trickle of foam lines his lips, the only visible sign of what they've done to him.

I press my palm against the glass partition, sick with

grief and horror and the knowledge that I can't reach him, can't help him, can't even close his eyes.

I back away from the glass, tears burning my eyes. There's nothing I can do for him now. But I can learn the truth about what they're doing here—what they might be planning to do to Henry and me.

As I slip out of the room, a cold certainty settles in my chest.

Eden isn't the paradise it seems.

TWENTY-NINE

HENRY

I check my watch again. 11:32 PM. Where is she?

I pace the length of our suite, my bare feet silent against the plush carpet that feels too soft, too luxurious for the knot of worry tightening in my chest. The balcony doors stand open, letting in the persistent sound of waves crashing against the shore.

Usually, it's calming. But tonight, it's just noise.

I shouldn't have walked out of that counseling session. I know that. But the look on Morgan's face when she accused Genevieve—wild, almost unhinged—it wasn't the woman I'd married. It was like watching a stranger wear her skin.

But she is just a stranger, isn't she?

No. I shake the voice off, not wanting to venture too deep in that direction of thought. Nothing good would come from it.

The bourbon burns as I swallow another mouthful. My third glass. Or fourth. I've lost count of them. The only reason I can keep count of the cigarettes I've smoked is by the fact that I had a fresh pack beforehand, and now it was empty. That was *twenty*, all smoked since I'd gotten back from the counseling session. It was excessive, even for me.

Perhaps I'd made a mistake and overreacted to the mention of this... Luka person. She'd just found a body, and the natural thing was to tell the authorities. If she'd made a friend out of one of the staff members, then could I really blame her for running to him?

Besides, what could I have done if she *did* come to me?

A heavy sigh escapes me as I drop onto the couch, leaning my head back against the cushion. Normally, it wasn't hard for me to stay angry, but for some reason, this time, it was. I suspected that reason was because the person I was angry at was her.

I glance at my watch again. A wave of worry passes through me.

"She's a grown woman," I mutter to myself, still holding the glass. "She's fine."

But I can't shake the feeling that something's wrong. Morgan's not the type to wander off like this. At least, I don't think so. We haven't really been in an argument like this before.

Not for the first time, I wish I could call her. But thanks to Eden, there are no phones on the resort, other than the one that's directly tied to the Eden reception. And quite frankly, they were the last people I wanted to speak with right now.

My mind drifts back to earlier, when Genevieve had shown up at our door, just twenty minutes after the disastrous counseling session. She was all smooth honey and smiles.

I'd stopped her at the threshold. "Not tonight, Eve."

"Henry," she'd said, her voice soft, like she was talking to a spooked animal. "I just want to make sure you're okay."

"I'm fine," I'd told her, not moving from the doorway. "Just need some time to process."

She'd leaned slightly forward, the smell of rose and musk wafting over me. As much as I hate to admit it, I loved the smell. It made me want to draw closer and breathe it in deeper.

And she knew it, judging by the coy smile that had spread across her lips.

"Don't you think you've had enough time, Henry?"

She really was crazy.

"I think we're done for tonight, Eve," I'd said, my voice firmer than I'd intended. "I appreciate your concern, but this is between me and my wife."

She hadn't backed away. Instead, she drew a step closer, closing the gap between us. She looked up at me with vulnerable eyes.

"Morgan means nothing. You know that. *I'm* your wife."

The way she'd said it, lingering a beat too long, sounded so pathetic and desperate. I'd been trying not to notice her attention, the way she looked at me from across the resort. But with her standing in front of me, she was doing her best to make it impossible to ignore.

I suddenly feel exhausted.

"Goodnight, Eve," I sighed, starting to close the door.

She'd paused, her eyes searching mine. "Goodnight, Henry. Remember, sometimes the people we love aren't who we think they are."

Now, hours later, those words still hang in the air like smoke.

I pour another drink, tossing it back in one burning swallow. What did she mean by that? Was she talking about Morgan? Or herself?

I'm overthinking this. It's late, I'm worried, and I'm letting my imagination run wild. Morgan will be back any minute now, and we'll talk this out like adults. I'll apologize for walking out. She'll apologize for lying and promise to never do it again, along with... well, being unhinged and making the wild accusation that Eve would *actually* kill someone. I'll ignore the whole Luka thing, and we'll move forward.

That's how it's supposed to work. Isn't it?

I think about the look in Dr. Warren's eyes when Morgan started her tirade. Not surprise. Not confusion. Something else. Something like...

A soft click interrupts my thoughts as the door unlocks. There's only one person with a keycard to the suite. Relief floods through me so intensely I almost stumble.

"Morgan," I start, ready to launch into the speech I've been rehearsing for hours.

But the words die in my throat when I see her face.

She's pale, her eyes wide and haunted. Her hands tremble as she closes the door behind her.

"What happened?" I ask, crossing the room to her. "Where have you been?"

She flinches when I reach for her, just slightly, but enough that I notice. Enough that it hurts.

"Morgan," I say again, gentler this time. "Talk to me."

She looks up at me, tears in her eyes. She opens her mouth to speak, but instead of words, a small, broken sound escapes.

"Hey," I say, guiding her to the bed. She's shaking so hard, I'm afraid she might collapse. "It's okay. You're okay now."

She shakes her head, tears spilling down her cheeks. "No," she whispers. "No, it's not okay. Nothing's okay."

I sit beside her, not touching her yet, giving her space. "Tell me what happened. Where were you?"

She looks at me, her eyes so filled with fear it makes my chest ache. But something else passes across her face —hesitation. Like she's weighing what to say.

"I just—" she starts, then stops, swallowing hard. "I need to get out of here, Henry. We need to leave. Please."

"Leave the resort? Now?"

"Yes," she says, her voice breaking on the word. "Now. Tonight."

I stare at her, searching for some explanation in her expression. "Morgan, it's the middle of the night. What happened?"

She looks away, her fingers twisting together in her lap. My eyes catch on the glint of the diamond ring I'd given her. This was my wife, and she needed me.

I press my hands over hers, lending her all the warmth I can give her.

She looks down at our hands, and after a moment,

says, "I can't—I can't tell you. Not right now. Please don't ask me to."

"You can't tell me?" I repeat, disbelief creeping into my voice. "You disappear for hours, come back looking like this, and say you can't tell me why?"

She turns back to me, and the raw fear in her eyes stops my next words cold.

"I'm sorry," she whispers, and it's so unlike her—this small, broken voice. "I'm so sorry. For everything. For what I said about Genevieve. For making you angry. I just —I need you to trust me. Please."

She reaches for my hand, her fingers ice-cold against my skin.

"I just want to be with you," she says, her voice child-like in its simplicity, in its desperation. "I just want us to go home. Please get us off this island, Henry. Please."

Though we'd only been together a short time, I've never seen her like this. I thought I knew her, inside and out. Sure, I knew that there were still parts of her that it would take me years to learn, but this trembling, pleading woman in front of me? I could've never pictured Morgan being like this.

And that terrifies me more than anything.

"Morgan," I say carefully. "Did someone hurt you?"

The thought makes my blood boil, and I suddenly know that I would be capable of murder if someone did.

She shakes her head quickly. "No. Not me. But we can't stay here. We can't."

I look at her, *really* look at her. Though I'd known that she was as desperate for this marriage as I was, not once had she ever begged me for anything.

This was serious.

This was like that first day I saw her, when she fell. This was the moment I could either step back and watch the marriage fall apart before it had a chance, or step up and offer her my hand.

The choice is obvious.

"Okay," I say, squeezing her hand. "Give me one day to make arrangements. I'll handle it."

I can tell she doesn't even want to wait a day, judging by the awful way she's trembling. But I gently press my fingers to her chin, tilting her face so that she can look into my eyes.

"Just one day, then we're out of here. You can even pack your bags now, if you like."

She closes her eyes, tears streaming down her cheeks. "We can't wait, Henry. It's not safe."

"I won't let anything happen to you," I whisper, finally pulling her into my arms. This time she doesn't resist, instead collapsing against me like she's been holding herself together by sheer will. "I promise. But we need to be smart about this."

She feels so small against me, so fragile. I think about how solid she usually is, how strong. This was the woman who'd chosen to confront Eve, of all people. Whatever happened tonight, it broke something in her.

"One day," I say again. "Just one day, and then we're gone."

She nods against my chest, clutching the fabric of my shirt. "Okay," she whispers. "One day."

"I'm sorry," she murmurs again, the words muffled against my chest. "I'm so sorry."

"Shh," I soothe, stroking her hair. "It's okay."

I hold her until her breathing evens out, until the trembling stops. I help her out of her clothes and into bed, pulling the covers up around her like I would for a child. She looks up at me, her eyes heavy with exhaustion and fear.

"Don't leave me," she says, her voice so quiet I almost don't hear it.

"Never," I promise, climbing into bed beside her. I pull her close, my arm around her waist, my chest against her back.

We lie there in the dark, both pretending to sleep. I have a thousand questions burning in my mind, but I know now isn't the time to push. Whatever has Morgan this terrified, she can't bring herself to tell me. Not yet.

I stare at the ceiling, listening to Morgan's shallow breathing beside me. I think about the look on Genevieve's face earlier today. The way she said, "Sometimes the people we love aren't who we think they are."

Morgan stirs, murmuring something I can't make out. I tighten my arm around her, as if I could protect her from whatever nightmares are chasing her.

One day, I told her. One day, and we'd be gone.

But as I lie here in the darkness, listening to the waves and Morgan's breathing, I can't shake the feeling it's already too late.

THIRTY
MORGAN

My eyes creak open, the morning light spilling through the half-drawn curtains, stabbing into the darkness. Normally, I hated being woken by the light. But this time, I'm grateful, because it's *finally* freed me from the nightmares.

I draw a deep breath, trying to still my pounding heart. Part of me wonders whether I imagined the last forty-eight hours, if Brody and Luka are both still walking around the resort somewhere.

The weight of dread sitting heavy in my stomach tells me otherwise.

No, this is reality.

And despite having never seen a dead body before, I've now witnessed two murdered men. I draw the blankets over my head like a child, as if cotton and thread could somehow protect me from Genevieve and Dexter and whoever else is out there to get me.

"Henry?" I call out tentatively, suddenly conscious of the empty space beside me.

Carefully, I peek out from under the blanket and scan the room. The dressing room light is on, but I know he's not in there. He has a habit of leaving it on after he's done. Which means he went somewhere.

Cold panic begins to slither down my spine. Did I tell Henry what happened last night?

I didn't.

Oh God, he doesn't know how dangerous Dexter is. He doesn't know how cold-blooded that monster is. What if he goes to him, tells him about the state I was in, and Dexter somehow realizes that I know about Luka? Dexter was sharp enough to tie my panic attack to the timing of Luka's murder.

Terror turns my blood to ice. I scramble out of bed and hear the crinkle of paper beneath my hand. Frowning, I look back and see a note that I hadn't noticed before.

It's from Henry.

Be back soon, my love. Gone for a morning jog. Will bring you breakfast if you wake up before I'm back.

He went for a morning jog? I shake my head in disbelief. When I'd first seen him, I thought that here was a man who embodied perfection, from his kind heart to the muscles rippling across his body. But I'm beginning to think that maybe his obsession with staying in shape isn't so perfect after all. But who am I to judge? Maybe it's his way of dealing with things.

I sigh and make my way to the bathroom, running cold water over my face. My reflection stares back at me from the mirror, green eyes hollow with dark shadows beneath them.

I wonder if I'll ever be the same after this trip. If I'll ever go back to being that innocent librarian who pined for love and knew nothing about the dark side of human nature. Somehow, I doubt it.

I just wish I knew why they killed him. What were they so afraid of Luka telling me?

My eyes close and I think back to his final moments. The fear in his eyes. The clinical detachment in the woman's voice as she administered the injection. The way Dexter spoke about storing the body, like he was discussing where to toss the trash.

"The answers you're looking for are going to be in your counselor's files, okay? You have to get to them."

Luka's words echo in my mind. There was something else he said, but the sudden sight of his empty eyes has me gasping and pulling myself out of the memory, splashing water over my face again like it would help.

I'm not sure why Dr. Warren's files matter, but after seeing what Dexter was capable of, I have to think that whatever Luka wants me to know is life or death.

I glance at the clock: 7:42 AM. Our next session isn't until 11:00. Henry's note said he'd bring breakfast, which means he probably won't be back for at least another half hour. The counseling building would be quiet this early, with most of the staff focused on breakfast service and morning activities.

This might be my only chance.

I move quickly, pulling on jeans and a light sweater, tying my hair back in a simple ponytail. No makeup—I don't have time, and besides, I need to look natural, like

I'm just out for an early morning walk. Nothing suspicious.

My hands tremble as I slip on my shoes. I'm about to break into my counselor's office. I'm about to rifle through confidential files. If I'm caught...

But if I don't do this, if I don't find out what's really happening here, Henry and I might never leave this island. At least not alive.

At the door, I hesitate. Should I leave Henry a note? Tell him where I've gone?

No. If I'm caught, it's better he doesn't know. Better he can honestly say he had no idea what I was doing. I need to protect him, even if he doesn't understand from what.

Besides, I don't want to lie to him again. Whatever Dr. Warren's sessions were worth, at least they taught me one thing: lying to Henry undermines our marriage, and I can't let that fall apart. It would completely and utterly ruin me.

I slip out of the suite, locking the door behind me. The morning air is cool against my skin, carrying the salt of the ocean and the sweetness of tropical flowers. It would be beautiful if I didn't know that people were being murdered here.

I keep my pace casual as I move through the resort grounds, nodding politely to the few early risers I pass. To them, I was just another guest enjoying the morning beauty of the resort, and nothing more.

My heart hammers in my chest as I pull on the door to the building, and pass through to the waiting area outside Dr. Warren's office. It's eerily quiet, which only makes the pounding of my heart seem so much louder.

Every instinct screams at me to turn around, to run back to the safety of our suite and let Henry sort things out. One day, and then we were gone. He'd promised, and he wasn't the kind of man who broke his promises.

But I keep going. For Luka. For Brody. For Henry and me.

Dr. Warren's office door is closed but, miraculously, unlocked. I slip inside, closing it softly behind me.

Wasting no time, I move to the far wall and the bookshelves lining them. I scan the spines of the books.

Psychology textbooks. Self-help manuals. Literary classics.

Then, I see it. Almost at eye level is a thin book, no wider than the width of my pinky: 'Paradise Lost' by Jeremy Milton.

My fingers brush against the spine, trembling slightly. It looks like any other book, but when I try to pull it from the shelf, it resists, then gives with a soft click.

The entire section of shelving swings outward an inch, revealing darkness beyond.

I glance back at the door, listening for any sound of approaching footsteps. Silence.

Taking a deep breath, I pull the hidden door wider, revealing a small cabinet built into the wall. Inside, organized in neat rows, are folders. Dozens of them, each labeled with names.

I scan them quickly, my heart pounding in my ears.

Anderson. Beshlie. Dominguez. Harris. James.

Langford.

My fingers close around the folder with our name on it, pulling it free. It's thicker than I expected, and inside the folder are a grouping of three smaller folders.

Henry. Morgan. And... Genevieve?

My breath catches in my throat. I place mine and Henry's folders on the table and reach for Genevieve's.

On the first page is a simple photograph of her. But it's not just a photograph of Genevieve. It's a photograph of Genevieve and Henry.

Together.

My fingers hover above the image, trembling. They're in what looks like a restaurant, candlelight catching the glint of their wine glasses. Henry's arm is draped around her shoulders. They're both smiling. Happy.

In love.

The date stamp on the bottom corner of the photo reads 04/17/2021. Just about four years ago.

"What the hell?" I whisper, my voice strange and distorted in the silent office.

I flip to the next page. It's a detailed psychological assessment, Dr. Warren's neat handwriting filling the margins with additional notes.

Genevieve Langford presents with understandable emotional distress following her separation from Henry. She shows remarkable commitment to healing their relationship, despite the pain. Her love for him remains profoundly intact.

Treatment approach: Facilitate meaningful reconciliation

through our marriage therapy program, preserving the core emotional bonds while eliminating destructive patterns.

I continue reading, my stomach turning with each sentence.

Session 3: Genevieve continues to maintain that Henry is "the love of her life" and is "willing to do whatever it takes" to rebuild their marriage. She has embraced the Eden Therapeutic Marriage Renewal Program fully after our discussions of the exceptional success rate. All consent forms completed.

Session 4: Genevieve expressed natural hesitation about the Stand-In component of therapy, particularly regarding Henry developing temporary intimacy with another woman. After our discussion about emotional recalibration and the transformative power of contrast, she has recommitted to the process.

Direct quote: "If this will make him remember why he fell in love with me, I'll do anything."

Note: Genevieve shows the exact emotional dedication we seek in our premium clients. Her ability to temporarily set aside jealousy for the greater goal of marriage restoration indicates excellent prognosis.

Eden Therapeutic Marriage Renewal Program?

My eyes dart to Henry's folder, but I hesitate. Luka told me something else... something about looking at

Henry's file specifically. I strain to remember his exact words.

"Don't bother with your files, or her's. Look for his."

But there was something else he'd said. A warning in his eyes that I hadn't fully understood in that moment.

"I told you. Nothing is what it seems."

With shaking hands, I ignore my folder and reach for Henry's, expecting to see another photograph when I open it.

But it's not.

It's a contract.

My eyes scan the title, printed in bold black letters across the top:

EDEN THERAPEUTIC MARRIAGE RENEWAL PROGRAM (TMRP): CLIENT AGREEMENT

Below that, Henry's signature, dated just two months ago.

I flip through the pages, words jumping out at me.

...our signature immersion therapy designed to revitalize exceptional marriages through guided emotional reconnection...

...the Stand-In Wife serves as a therapeutic mirror, allowing the Client and Original Wife to rediscover their capacity for intimacy and commitment...

...all emotional journey components are carefully curated

to ensure the Client experiences profound trans-
formation...

...upon completion of the healing journey, Client will be
reunited with their Original Partner with renewed appre-
ciation and deeper emotional connection.

My brain struggles to make sense of what I'm reading, to connect these phrases to the life I've been living. To the man I've been loving.

I turn back to the first page, and that's when I see it. A section labeled "Therapeutic Participants," with three lines:

Client: *Henry James Langford*
Original Wife: *Genevieve Marie Langford*
Stand-In Wife: *Morgan Sloane*

Stand-In Wife.
That's me.
That's what I am.
A substitute. A therapeutic tool. A human placebo.
"No," I whisper, flipping through more pages. "No, no, no."
I find a section titled "Therapeutic Journey" and force myself to read it.

Phase 1: Selection and Preparation (Complete)
Stand-In carefully matched to Client's emotional needs
and attachment patterns.

Phase 2: Orchestrated Beginning (Complete)
"Marriage at First Sight" immersion experience initiated.

Phase 3: Guided Emotional Rebirth (In Progress)
Eden resort therapeutic environment with controlled emotional catalysts.

Phase 4: Reintegration (Pending)
Client reunion with Original Wife following vow renewal.

Phase 5: Completion (Pending)
Stand-In transition and aftercare protocol.

Stand-In transition? What does that even mean?

I push Henry's folder aside and reach for mine with numb fingers. Unlike the others, it's thin, almost empty.

The first page has my photo—the professional headshot from my library's website. There were other photos of me too: one where I'm watching TV in my apartment, another one where I'm working in the library, and... am I getting out of the shower in this one?

I feel sick. How did they even get these, with how fast they'd contacted me after I submitted my application?

I quickly flip to the next page. Unlike Genevieve's detailed assessments, my file contains only brief, clinical notes.

Morgan Sloane selected for Stand-In Wife, with a high quality profile. Has displayed desperateness, romantic idealism, and loneliness due to lack of personal connec-

tions, both family and professional. Exhibits multiple
vulnerability markers.

Susceptibility to Eden narrative: Very High.
Ideal Candidate Status: Confirmed.

They chose me because of how desperate I was for
love.

Because I would believe a fairy tale about marrying a
perfect stranger.

I flip through more pages, finding session notes from
Dr. Warren.

Stand-In continues to develop authentic attachment to
Client, demonstrating ideal emotional mirroring. Her
natural insecurities about the Original Wife create
productive tension that reinforces Client's protective
instincts.

Her willingness to adapt herself (perfume change, hair-
style modification) mirrors Original Wife's key traits,
creating memory moments for Client.

Remains fully immersed in therapeutic narrative.

They've been using me. Using my love, my devotion,
my entire being as a tool to make Henry fall back in love
with his real wife.

With Genevieve.

I turn to the final page in my folder, and my blood
freezes in my veins.

Stand-In Completion Protocol: Transition date adjusted to coincide with program finale. Client displaying all benchmark behaviors indicating readiness for reunion with Original Wife. Standard elimination procedures to follow, with complete removal of all Stand-In evidence from Client's experience.

Elimination procedures.

They're going to kill me.

Just like they killed Luka.

My hands are shaking so badly now that I can barely hold the pages. My stomach heaves, and for a moment I think I might actually vomit right here on Dr. Warren's pristine carpet.

I force myself to breathe, to think.

This doesn't make sense. Henry loves me. I know he does. I've seen it in his eyes, felt it in his touch. That can't all be fake. It can't.

I flip back to Henry's file, searching for something, anything that might tell me his true feelings. But there's nothing.

Did I have it wrong this whole time?

My heart says no. But my mind hesitates. The entire time we've been here, Henry has insisted that Genevieve was just a stalker, that she was insignificant and that I was everything.

But that was a lie... He's been lying to me, using me all this time.

A sound from the outer office freezes me in place. Voices. Someone's coming.

Frantically, I begin gathering the papers, shoving

them back into their respective folders. My hands are clumsy with panic, and a page from my file slips free, floating to the floor.

The voices are getting closer.

I snatch up the paper, stuff it and the folders back into the hidden cabinet, and push the bookshelf back into place. It clicks shut just as the office door begins to open.

There's nowhere to hide except—

I dive under Dr. Warren's desk, curling myself into the smallest ball possible, praying that whoever has entered won't need to sit down.

"We can speak in here," Dr. Warren says.

"You're not concerned that the attachment is too strong?" Dexter asks.

"It's a natural part of the process." Dr. Warren's voice is calm, reassuring. "The deeper his connection to the Stand-In, the more profound his emotional revival will be when he reunites with Genevieve."

"He's asked to meet with me, suggesting that he wants to move the timeline of the completion up to tomorrow."

"That's excellent progress. I assume you're aware of what occurred just yesterday?"

"Only partially."

"Henry reassured Genevieve. He chose her over Morgan in a moment of conflict. That alone is a break-through indicator. But even beyond that, he's been unconsciously recreating Genevieve through Morgan—having her wear the same hairstyle, the same perfume from when they first met."

Dexter doesn't say anything, seemingly hesitant.

"He still calls her 'Eve' in his private moments."

Dexter sighs. "Okay, I trust your expert opinion. And the Stand-In? Any complications there?"

"Elevated anxiety, as expected. She isn't a concern."

My heart pounds so hard I'm certain they must hear it.

"Alright. Then I will plan on granting Henry his request to move the completion up to tomorrow night. Ideally, I would feel more comfortable with the original established timeline, but if he and Genevieve are ready for their reunion, then it's our duty to facilitate that."

"Excellent. I look forward to witnessing another Eden success story," Dr. Warren says, sounding genuinely pleased.

"As do I."

The door opens and closes. I strain to hear if anyone remains in the room, but it seems quiet. Even so, I wait another full minute before uncurling my cramped limbs and peering out from under the desk.

The office is empty.

I crawl out, my entire body trembling. It takes three tries to stand, my legs weak beneath me.

Tomorrow night.

I have until tomorrow night to escape, or I'll be killed and no doubt dumped next to Luka and Brody's bodies. The thought nearly paralyzes me, but I know that I have to get out of here while I can.

Moving to the door, I press my ear against it.

Nothing.

I crack it open and peer out. The waiting area is still empty.

I slip out of the office and hurry down the hallway,

my mind racing, the reality of my situation still crashing over me like a tidal wave, threatening to drown me.

The seemingly perfect life I was about to have was just a lie. My marriage. My husband. My future.

I'm not Henry's wife. I'm a psychological tool designed to reopen his heart so he can love his real wife again.

I'm disposable.

And in a way, I'm already dead.

I stumble out of the building into the bright morning sunlight, the beauty of the day a mockery of the darkness I've discovered. Couples stroll by, holding hands, smiling, unaware that they're walking past a woman whose world has just been obliterated.

Are they real? Or are they like me—pawns in some sick game they don't understand?

I have a gut feeling that all of this is orchestrated purely for Henry and Genevieve. These other couples might be real, not just actors playing their parts, but nobody here is going to save me.

I need to think. I need to plan. But my mind keeps circling back to one devastating truth: the man I love has never been mine. And by design, he never will be.

A shadow falls across my path, and I look up.

"There you are." Henry smiles, holding a paper bag. "I brought breakfast. Are you feeling better this morning?"

I stare at him, really seeing him for the first time. Not my husband. A client in a twisted therapy program. A man who came to this island to remember how to love someone else.

"Morgan?" His smile falters. "What's wrong?"

Everything is wrong. Everything has always been wrong.

But I force my lips into a smile, even as my heart shatters into a thousand irreparable pieces.

"Nothing," I lie. "I'm just glad to see you."

Because the truth is too terrible to say out loud. The truth is that I've been living in a beautiful lie, constructed with painstaking care by people who saw me as disposable.

I've been reading the wrong story all along. This isn't a fairy tale about finding love. It's a story about fixing something broken.

As Henry's fingers brush mine while handing me the breakfast bag, I wonder if he knows. If somewhere deep inside, behind those loving eyes that I've trusted completely, he's always known that I was just temporary. That I was never meant to survive this "therapy."

Something tells me he does.

THIRTY-ONE
MORGAN

The infinity pool water laps against my feet, cool and deceptive like everything else in this place. Above me, stars blanket the sky in a display so perfect it could only be fake.

Like my marriage. Like my husband. Like my entire life.

Henry sleeps inside our suite, oblivious. I waited until his breathing deepened, then slipped outside, needing space to think.

With no way off the island, I have less than twenty-four hours to live.

The thought should terrify me. But after spending the rest of the day pretending—smiling at Henry over dinner and kissing my husband goodnight—I've gone numb.

I stare at my rippling reflection in the dark water.

Who is that woman?

The naive librarian who believed in love at first sight is gone. Dead already. In her place is someone harder.

Someone who knows that monsters don't lurk in the pages of gothic novels, but behind pleasant smiles in paradise.

Before she passed, my mother said that when people die, they become stars. I glance up, imagining her looking down on me right now.

Would she be disappointed to see the hole I'd dug for myself?

I scoff, splashing the water gently with a wave of my foot. She shouldn't be. After all, she was the one who married my father. Not like she did any better than me.

Either way, I suppose I'll know tomorrow night, when I take my own place among the stars. A single tear rolls down my cheek as I realize that there'll be nobody to mourn my disappearance. Tiana will think I've either run off with my husband, all happy and giddy, or been murdered. Either way, she'll be able to prove nothing and will eventually just move on with her life. As for anybody else...

"So, objectively, you are alone."

Dexter's voice suddenly whispers through my mind. They'd planned for this, made sure to select someone for Henry who wouldn't be missed.

And Henry...

My chest aches. Was any of it real? The way he looked at me, touched me, held me? Or was it all just his body going through the motions while his heart prepared to return to Genevieve?

I draw my knees to my chest, angry at myself for still caring. Still hoping that somehow, his feelings for me were genuine.

It doesn't matter. I saw the contract. His signature was on it, right next to Genevieve's. He knew I was temporary, disposable.

A Stand-In Wife.

The beautiful resort around me—just stage dressing for a sick experiment in emotional manipulation. The perfect setting for the perfect victim.

Me.

I wasn't chosen because I was *special*. I was chosen because I was lonely. Vulnerable. Desperate enough to believe in an impossible dream.

The realization burns, stripping away the last of my last illusions. I've spent my entire life waiting for someone to choose me, to make me the center of their world.

And now, the crowning achievement of my pathetic existence: I was so eager to be chosen that I fell for an elaborate scam designed to exploit that very desperation.

More tears fall.

I look away from my own reflection, knowing what I'll see: a pathetic person who still loves Henry, who would give anything to not know what I know now.

That's the worst part: I'd still choose the beautiful lie over this humiliating reality. But I don't get to choose. I never did.

The stars continue their cold twinkling, unmoved by my tragedy. Eden continues its paradise charade. None of it cares that my world has ended.

I wonder how many women sat here before me, realizing too late they'd been used as emotional training wheels. How many are buried somewhere on this island?

A shooting star streaks across the sky. I don't bother making a wish. I'm done with wishes. Done with hoping someone else will save me.

Instead, I make a promise.

I may die tomorrow, but I'm not going to go to the grave without ruining the Eden fantasy. Henry and Genevieve Langford want their happily ever after?

Well, they're not getting it.

"Genevieve!"

She doesn't hear me. Or maybe she does and just doesn't care. The wind carries my voice away as I jog across the uneven sand, my breath already coming short. A few couples glance our way, but I ignore them, pushing forward.

I'm not built for this kind of chase. I'm a librarian, for God's sake. Very few moments in my life have required me to shout, let alone sprint down a beach after a murderer.

Still, I try again. "Genevieve!"

No response. She walks ahead, stripping away layers, revealing that frustratingly perfect body, her model-ready bikini practically sculpted to her form. She looks like she's about to swim.

And that's a problem.

I pick up the pace despite the wheezing in my chest. I have no desire to chase her into the ocean, where she'd have every advantage over me. Drowning me would be effortless. Not that she needs to do the dirty work herself. Eden's already marked me for elimination.

So, I change tactics.

"Eve!"

That gets her attention. Her head snaps around, eyes searching—expecting Henry. I feel the knife twist in my gut, but I snuff it out. No distractions. I have to stay focused.

Her gaze lands on me, and even from this distance, I see the flicker of disappointment. The way her body stiffens. The way she goes cold. She crosses her arms as I reach her, bent over and panting.

"Sorry, sorry," I gasp. "The sand... not exactly easy to run on."

She says nothing. Just looks at me like I'm something she stepped in.

"What is it you want, Morgan?"

I straighten, locking eyes with her. It takes everything I have not to clench my fists, not to let my frustration bleed through. She can't suspect me. Not yet. Instead, I force a smile—one that, with effort, reaches my eyes.

"Look, I just..." I wave a hand between us, as if that means something. "I think we got off on the wrong foot."

Her eyes narrow. She's suspicious, of course. And why shouldn't she be? This is coming from the woman who accused her of murder and tried to have her thrown off the resort.

She scans the beach to see if anyone's watching. And then, just loud enough for only me to hear, she says, "You're worried I'm going to kill you."

A laugh bubbles out of me before I can stop it. A little too real. "I was," I admit. "But I don't think you will."

"And why is that?"

Because I know you don't have to. Because Eden already has plans to get rid of me, though I'm sure you'd enjoy doing it yourself.

The thought sends a shiver down my spine, but I bury it deep. Instead, I fidget with the hem of my sundress. "Just a feeling."

She doesn't look convinced.

I sigh, shifting tactics. "Look, I'm not going to stand here and pretend I understand what happened with Brody. But quite frankly? It's not my business."

"Didn't seem that way when you were screaming bloody murder, trying to get me thrown off the resort."

"Can you blame me?" I let out a small, self-depre-cating laugh. "I'm a jealous cow."

She blinks. A crack in the armor.

I throw everything at it.

"You're beautiful. Smart. It's easy to see why Henry chose you in the first place." I let my voice catch, just slightly, on the word *wife*. "But honestly? I'm not mad at you. If anything, I like you."

The lies taste like salt on my tongue, but I swallow them.

"I've realized something," I say. "We're really the same."

Her brow lifts. But the cold edge in her expression softens. "We're the same?"

"We both love him. And we're both stuck in this

awful situation where... I don't know." I force my shoulders to slump slightly, like I'm defeated. "You know?"

She studies me, eyes sharp, like she's trying to peel back my skin and see what's underneath.

"Why are you doing this?" she asks at last.

I hesitate, just enough to make it believable. "Eden's moving up our departure date. We're leaving tonight. And I don't want to leave with this tension between us. Especially since..." I let the words trail, let them seem difficult to say. "Since we'll probably still be in each other's lives. Henry loves me. But I think he still loves you too. I've seen the way he looks at you when you're not looking. And the fact that he still calls you Eve..."

The words burn coming out, but I keep my expression resigned. Like I'm making peace with it.

"I just thought," I continue, "if we're going to be connected after all this, maybe we could try not to hate each other?"

She watches me for a long, long moment.

"Why are you *really* doing this, Morgan?" Her voice is soft but sharp, like the edge of a paper cut.

I let her see just enough real emotion to be convincing. Pain. Betrayal. Fear. All of it is right there beneath my skin, so I don't have to reach far.

"Because fighting is exhausting."

My hands tremble slightly, and I don't have to fake that either. Standing this close to her makes my skin crawl.

She exhales through her nose. "You know," she muses, "I think I have the wrong impression of you."

"I guess we don't really know each other," I say,

putting on my best fake smile. "Maybe when this is all over, we could... I don't know. Get coffee or something."

She looks at me like I just suggested we go swimming with sharks. "Not a good idea."

I blink, glancing away, like I'm hurt.

"But I'll think about it."

I school my expression. "Good. Look, I should go. I want to prepare something special for when Henry gets back to the suite to pack. Last day on the resort and all."

Jealousy flashes across her face, sharp and ugly.

"Maybe you want to join us?" I add, feigning innocence.

Her expression shutters, confusion mixing with something unreadable. She stammers and shakes her head.

I sigh, reaching out to squeeze her hand. "Then I'll see you after all this."

Then I turn before she can respond, walking back up the beach, every step measured. When I glance over my shoulder, I see her gathering her clothes, stamping back toward her suite.

A slow grin curls my lips.

Things are going exactly as planned.

THIRTY-THREE
MORGAN
THIRTY MINUTES EARLIER

The sunlight is relentless as I duck behind the thick cluster of bougainvillea surrounding Genevieve's suite. My heart is racing so hard I worry she might actually hear it through the open window.

I'm getting too familiar with the feeling of being someplace I shouldn't be, pressed against the side of the building, hoping to remain unnoticed. But desperate times and all that.

Through the partially open window, I can see Genevieve moving around inside her suite. Genevieve—the woman who has made my life hell since she arrived, the woman Henry married first, the woman who killed Brody and walked away as if it never happened.

And right now, she's *humming*.

The carefree tune drifts toward me, a light melody I vaguely recognize but can't place. My jaw clenches as I watch her get ready, changing outfits multiple times, studying her reflection critically in the mirror. I'm beginning to wonder how long she's going to take, when finally, she settles on a bikini covered loosely by a gauzy sundress, twirling one last time in front of the mirror.

She looks like she's getting ready for someone. Henry, probably, in the hopes that she'd see him on the beach.

She disappears into the bathroom, and moments later, the shower starts running. Steam drifts out the window, carrying the scent of coconut shampoo. It smells expensive, luxurious—like everything else about her.

I hesitate only for a second before going to the front door and quickly tapping in the key code, holding my breath in hopes that it hadn't been changed yet.

There *was* one lucky thing in all of this for me—with the resort being full and every suite being taken, there were no other rooms for Genevieve to be switched to after the staff found the body. Instead, they'd cleaned it thoroughly and apologized profusely. But in all honesty, having seen how she was content to leave Brody's body beneath that water, I don't think it mattered.

The light flashes green, and I breathe a sigh of relief, slipping inside.

The suite is cool, the air-conditioned breeze hitting me as I step inside. Immediately, I'm hit by the scent of Genevieve's perfume. My stomach turns, reminding me of how much I was beginning to hate that smell.

Just as before, her room is immaculate. It looks like nothing's been moved, with the exception of one addition: a framed photo on the bedside table—Genevieve and Henry on their wedding day. His arms wrapped around her waist, their smiles radiant, eyes locked lovingly.

I hate that it still hurts to see it.

The shower water abruptly shuts off, jolting me back into action. I pull out the carefully forged note from my pocket. I'd painstakingly copied Henry's handwriting, each curve and letter carefully rehearsed until it looked undeniably genuine.

I glance around the room for the best place to leave the note. Somewhere that she won't notice, not until she returns from the beach. My eyes fall on the table, where the flowers are. I slide the note beside it. Easy enough to see when you enter, but invisible when you leave.

I just had to hope that she didn't look back when she left.

The bathroom door clicks.

Panic spikes through me. I bolt for the front door, my steps muffled by thick carpeting. Behind me, I hear Eve humming again, blissfully unaware of how close she was to catching me. My pulse thunders as I ease the door shut behind me.

I sprint around the corner of the building, pressing my back against the wall as I catch my breath. One minute later, Eve emerges from her suite, her expression relaxed, oblivious. She heads toward the beach, her stride easy, like everything was going right in the world.

And for her, it *was*. For whatever reason, Brody was dead and out of the way with nobody suspecting her, and after tonight, Henry would be back with her, their vows reaffirmed and their connection rekindled.

My hands are trembling—not from fear, oddly, but from something else. Something like exhilaration. Funny how fear fades when you know you're going to die anyway. There's a strange freedom in it.

I give Genevieve a few minutes before I follow, thinking about the message on the note. I wish I could be there to see her face when she reads it, but it's best for me to be someplace else.

It's best for me to be with her lovely Henry.

Counting down the seconds, I finally head for the beach. She's far ahead, but I can still catch her if I run.

"Genevieve!"

THIRTY-FOUR
GENEVIEVE

I storm back to my suite, sand still clinging between my toes, that encounter with Morgan replaying in my mind. The nerve of that woman. Her pathetic attempt at making peace, suggesting we get coffee, like we're sorority sisters catching up after graduation.

The thought of that is laughable. She wants to be friends after all this, like she hasn't been trying to steal my husband from me? And what was that at the end, inviting me to join her with *my own husband?*

The very thought makes my skin crawl.

Morgan was so painfully obvious. So transparent in her desperation, it was almost embarrassing to watch. The way she spoke to me on the beach, pretending to surrender to me and accept that she might have to share Henry with me—it was all a performance. A badly executed one at that. Does she think I'm stupid?

I have to admit, watching the little librarian play at being sophisticated and worldly amused me.

The suite welcomes me with its cool air, the scent of expensive room spray, and perfect silence. I kick off my sandals, feeling the plush carpet beneath my feet, and head straight for the shower, despite the fact that I'd taken one not just thirty minutes ago.

There's sand sticking to my calves, my thighs. I hate that—the way it clings, refuses to let go. Like Morgan.

The warm water washes over me, and I close my eyes, letting myself imagine how tonight will play out. Henry will finally come back to me. We'll restart our life together. This resort and the past few years will fade like a bad dream, and everything will be as it should be.

As we always planned.

I step out of the shower, wrapping myself in one of the resort's impossibly soft towels. My reflection stares back at me—all high cheekbones and sharp eyes, the kind of beauty that takes work to maintain. Not like Morgan's effortless, girl-next-door look. The kind men find "refreshing," until they realize there's *nothing* beneath the surface.

I've put in the work. Endured the pain. I've earned this.

Padding back into the bedroom, I notice something new. A folded piece of paper by the bouquet of fresh flowers. I frown. The housekeeping staff usually leaves notes on the desk, not by the flowers.

But then my heart quickens as I recognize the handwriting on the front.

Henry.

I snatch up the note, a small smile playing at my lips.

He must have slipped in while I was at the beach. Before we had our issues, he was always the romantic, leaving little gifts for me everywhere. It's one of the things I've always loved about him.

My fingers unfold the paper slowly, savoring the moment. The last note before our reunion. A memento I'll keep to remind us both of how far we've come.

But as my eyes scan the words, my smile fades, replaced by cold disbelief.

Eve,

I've been trying to find the right words, the right moment. There isn't one. So I'm writing this instead.

Eden promised they could fix us. Promised I could remember why we fell in love in the first place. And for a while, I thought it was working. Being with Morgan was supposed to be temporary—a way to relearn what we'd lost.

But something unexpected happened. Something I never planned for.

I've come to want her. Not as a substitute. Not as a reflection of you. But as herself.

I know this isn't what we agreed to. I know this betrays everything we came here for. But I can't lie to you anymore. I can't lie to myself.

What we had was beautiful once. But it's over. It's been over for longer than either of us wanted to admit.

I'm sorry, Eve.

Please don't try to contact me. It's better this way.

Goodbye,
Henry

The paper trembles in my hands. This isn't happening. This can't be happening.

"Liar!" I scream, ripping the note in half, then quarters, then eighths until my fingers can tear no more. "LIAR!"

I hurl the pieces across the room, watching them scatter like confetti. Like the remains of my life.

My legs give way beneath me, and I sink to the floor, the plush carpet catching me. My hands shake uncontrollably, my breath coming in short, ragged gasps.

This isn't right. This isn't how it's supposed to go.

Henry wouldn't do this. He couldn't. We have a contract. We have an agreement.

A sob tears from my throat, raw and ugly. Followed by another. And another. Until I'm rocking back and forth, clutching myself, drowning in the tidal wave of betrayal.

After everything I've done. After everything I've endured.

The embarrassment of our separation. The indignity and pain of watching him waltz around the resort with another woman, as Eden's therapists assured me this was all part of the process.

I trusted them. I trusted *him*.

And now he wants to leave with *her*? That pathetic little nothing who couldn't hold a man's attention for five minutes?

I drag myself to my feet, stumbling to the bathroom. My reflection stares back at me—mascara streaking down my cheeks, eyes red and swollen. I look deranged. Broken.

I slam my fist into the mirror.

The glass spiderwebs around my knuckles, droplets of blood forming where shards pierce skin. The pain is clarifying, sharpening my thoughts.

Henry doesn't get to decide this.

Despite Henry being the official Client, I was the one who found Eden, who agreed to their terms. I *own* this outcome.

I rinse my bleeding hand under cold water, watching red swirl down the drain. The physical pain is nothing compared to what's raging inside me.

Years of marriage. Years of building a life together. And he thinks he can throw it all away for some slutty librarian? A woman selected precisely because she'd believe any fairy tale fed to her?

I wrap a washcloth around my hand, pressing hard to stop the bleeding.

The rage bubbling inside me transforms into something colder, more focused. More dangerous.

I glance toward the bathtub, where I'd finally gotten tired of that ridiculous man, Brody, and drowned him—all to keep from hearing his voice again.

I turn back to the torn pieces of the note, studying Henry's handwriting. There's no mistake. This is him—the specific way he curves his y's, the pressure points in his signature. The note is genuine.

But how could he do this? How could he walk away from everything we've built? Everything we've sacrificed for?

Unless Morgan somehow got to him. Manipulated him. Made him believe he loved her when it was all just part of the therapy.

That must be it. She's unknowingly turned the program against us, somehow convinced him that what he feels for her is real when it's nothing more than a psychological experiment working exactly as designed.

My Henry would never betray me like this. Not the man who proposed under the Northern Lights in Iceland. Not the man who held me through three miscarriages, promising we'd find our way through the darkness together.

I walk to the closet, pulling out my suitcase. Inside, nestled between layers of silk and cashmere, is a small leather case. I unzip it carefully, revealing the small handgun inside.

Eden assured me, over and over, that this process was tried and tested, with an incredible success rate. But I'd learned a long time ago that I needed to be prepared for all contingencies. I needed my own insurance, so to speak. A failsafe, in case this all went wrong.

I wasn't supposed to need this. The process was meant to be seamless. Perfect.

But Morgan has forced my hand.

I tuck the gun into my purse. I won't use it. Not yet. First, I need to talk to Henry. Look into his eyes. Remind him of who we are together. Of what we've survived.

He'll remember. He has to.

I pick up a larger shard of the broken mirror, holding it up and fixing my makeup with practiced precision. Erasing all evidence of tears. Of weakness. By the time I'm done, I'm flawless again. Composed. In control.

I slip into a white dress—Henry's favorite. The one I wore on our first anniversary, when he told me I was the only woman he'd ever love.

He meant it then. He means it now, whether he remembers it or not.

I check my reflection one final time, adjusting a strand of hair. Perfect.

I know exactly where he'll be. With her. In that suite they've been sharing, probably packing for tonight.

My fingers curl around my purse, feeling the outline of the gun through the leather.

As I step out into the hallway, Dr. Warren's voice slithers through my mind: *"Remember our discussion about extreme emotional response. Breathe. Center your-self. Trust the process."*

I kill the thought. There is no more process. No more trust.

There's only Henry, and me, and the vows we made to each other. Till death do us part.

And one way or another, I will honor those vows tonight.

THIRTY-FIVE
MORGAN

The shadows stretch long across our suite as the sun begins its descent. I sit on the edge of the bed, watching dust motes dance in the golden light filtering through the half-drawn curtains. My nerves are electric, my body restless.

Everything I've learned—the carefully constructed lie of my life, my impending death, the betrayal of the man I love—it should crush me. It should leave me paralyzed. Instead, I feel strangely alive. Present in a way I've never been before.

Maybe that's what imminent death does to you. Sharpens your senses. Makes you savor each moment.

The door clicks, and Henry walks in, his smile warming when he sees me. In his hands are two glasses filled with some tropical concoction, garnished with pineapple and tiny paper umbrellas. So perfectly on-brand for this place. For our fabricated paradise.

"Hey, you," he says, kicking the door shut behind him.

"They were making these at the bar. Thought you could use a drink before we start packing."

I take the glass without a word, setting it on the night-stand untouched. His eyes follow the movement, a slight frown creasing his brow.

"Everything okay?" he asks.

I look at him—really look at him. The man I married. The man I've spent months loving with every fiber of my being. The man who signed a contract agreeing to my eventual murder.

Is he acting right now? Is he genuinely concerned, or is this just another performance before the final curtain call?

It doesn't matter. Not anymore.

"Come here," I say, my voice low and steady.

His frown deepens, but he approaches, setting his own drink beside mine. I reach for him, pulling him down until our faces are inches apart. His eyes search mine, confused but curious.

"Morgan, what—"

I silence him with a kiss.

Not sweet. Not gentle. But desperate and demand-ing. The kiss of a woman with nothing left to lose.

For a moment, he's startled, but then he responds, so perfectly attentive.

Is that in the Eden handbook too? A checklist for making your Stand-In Wife fall helplessly in love with you?

I don't want to think about that. Not now. I push the thought away, focusing instead on the warmth of his skin, the familiar scent of his cologne, the way my body still responds to his touch despite everything I now know.

"I need you," I whisper against his mouth. "Right now."

Something dark and hungry flashes in his eyes— desire mixed with something else. Surprise, maybe. I've never been this forward, this urgent.

But I'm not the Morgan he married anymore. The last of that naive, trusting woman died in Dr. Warren's office, buried under the weight of contracts and psychological assessments.

He doesn't protest as I pull him toward the bed. As we move, falling into each other and ourselves, I watch his face, memorizing every detail. The way his eyelashes cast shadows on his cheeks. The slight scar at his temple from a childhood accident. The way his lips part.

Was any of it real? Any of the tenderness? The affection? The love?

I want to believe it was. Need to believe it, even now.

Outside, the sun sinks lower, painting our bodies in amber and gold, then deep red. Somewhere in the back of my mind, I register the symbolism.

One last sunset for Morgan and Henry. A final act of intimacy before the curtain falls on this manufactured marriage.

My breath catches, but not from pleasure. From the sudden, overwhelming realization that this is goodbye. Not just to Henry, but to the woman I was. The woman who believed in fairy tales and happily-ever-afters. The woman who thought she'd finally been chosen.

"I love you," Henry murmurs against my neck.

The words pierce me like a dagger. How easy they fall from his lips. How genuine they sound.

"Say it again," I demand, voice breaking despite my effort to stay composed. "Louder."

He pulls back slightly, eyes dark and intense in the fading light. "I love you, Morgan."

I stare into those eyes—the eyes I've trusted completely—searching for deceit. For calculation. For any sign that he's reading from Eden's script.

But there's only warmth and devotion staring back at me.

The world's greatest actor, and the perfect match to his perfectly manipulative wife, Genevieve.

I pull him back to me.

Let this be my farewell to the dream. To the fantasy that someone could love me completely, unconditionally. That I could be someone's first choice.

A prickling sensation crawls up the back of my neck, and I have the strangest sense we're not alone. That someone is *watching*.

My eyes dart to the window, searching the gathering darkness beyond.

Nothing. Just the night settling over the resort.

But the feeling persists. Intensifies.

And I know. I know with absolute certainty that she's out there.

Genevieve.

I close my eyes and surrender to the moment, knowing that it's all going as planned, and that the perfect ending they both envisioned would die a fiery death.

Let Henry believe the passion. Let Genevieve watch and feel her heart break. Let Eden think their plans are going well.

Let them all believe what they need to believe.

Because tonight, I know it'll all change.

As we collapse together in the half-light, Henry's weight comforting and familiar against me, I stare up at the ceiling. In my mind, I say goodbye to the woman who arrived on this island filled with hope and dreams. The librarian who believed she'd found her storybook ending.

"You're different tonight," Henry murmurs, his fingers tracing lazy patterns on my skin.

I turn to look at him, allowing myself one last moment of pretend. One final act of loving this man who was never truly mine.

"Just savoring our last moment in paradise," I say, the half-truth bitter on my tongue.

He smiles, kissing my forehead with such tenderness that my eyes burn with unshed tears. "We'll come back someday. When all this is behind us."

I force a smile, though my heart is breaking all over again. "I'd like that."

The prickling sensation returns, stronger now. My eyes are drawn to the window again, to the darkness beyond the glass. Is that a shadow moving? A face peering in?

"I should shower," I say, extracting myself from his embrace. "Dexter said he'd knock around seven to get us ready for the vows at ten."

Henry props himself up on one elbow, watching me

gather my discarded clothes. "I wonder why they decided to hold it all so late."

I shrug, unable to take any pleasure in how he still thinks I'm the dutiful, believing Stand-In Wife. The perfect, pliable Morgan who never questions, who trusts implicitly.

If only he knew the monster he'd created. The woman who now plots and schemes and lies as easily as she once loved.

As I step into the bathroom and close the door behind me, I catch one last glimpse of Henry in the bed we've shared. He looks peaceful. Content. Oblivious to the storm that's coming.

I turn on the shower, letting the water drown out the sound of my ragged breathing. Letting it wash away the tears that finally fall.

Outside, in the thickening darkness, I know Genevieve is watching. Waiting. Planning.

And now all I have to do is wait.

And let her be my deliverance of ruin.

THIRTY-SIX
GENEVIEVE

Did he just say he *loves* her?

THIRTY-SEVEN
MORGAN

I'm back in front of the mirrors where I'd first tried on my wedding dress. The soft, flattering lights dance across my reflection, designed to make every bride feel beautiful. But this time, I'm wearing a far simpler dress—one selected for the vow renewal ceremony.

One that I would wear to the grave.

It was chosen for me, like everything else in this cursed place. Though I objectively love the dress—the delicate lace overlay, the way it skims my body just so—I wish I'd chosen it myself. I would have liked to have worn something else to die in. Something that would have suited my mother's tastes instead of my own, so that when I ascend to the stars and join her, she would smile when she saw me.

Behind me, the consultant smiles with practiced enthusiasm while Dexter studies me with a curious, calculating eye. He knows something is wrong. Probably because I haven't said a word to him since he knocked on my door to escort me here. The silence between us stretches, long and heavy.

Judging by the slight furrow in his brow, he can't quite put his finger on what's changed. I know I should be smiling, maintaining the mask for as long as possible to avoid getting killed prematurely. But I can't bring myself to do it. After all, what's the difference between dying now and dying in a couple of hours? The countdown has already begun.

Dexter dismisses the consultant with a subtle nod. The door clicks shut, leaving me alone with him. He joins me at my side, our reflections standing together in the mirror—the executioner beside his victim.

"You're beautiful," he says, his voice smooth as always.

I nod quietly, watching him in the mirror rather than turning to face him directly.

"Are you afraid?" he asks.

My gaze snaps to his, wondering at the double-edged question. Did he mean if I was afraid of dying, or if I was afraid of going off with Henry? Is this some kind of test?

His face remains too stoic to read, a perfect mask crafted from years of professional detachment.

"A little," I admit, letting a fragment of truth seep into my words.

A beat passes before he nods, seeming satisfied with my answer. "It is normal, you know. Many of our Eden matches have expressed some sort of hesitation at this moment, before the completion of our program." His voice takes on that practiced therapeutic cadence I've come to despise. "But it's important to remember that you are already married to him. The hard part is already done, and all that's left is to live your life."

Live my life.

The irony would be almost laughable if it weren't so grotesque.

I hold his gaze in the mirror, studying his face more intently than I've ever done before. It's difficult to discern at first, hidden behind the professional stoicism and polite smiles. But there is an undeniable coldness there, behind his practiced warm eyes, that reveals the truth.

He sees me as a tool—something to be used and discarded once I've served my purpose. I wonder how many poor girls he has duped into traveling across the world to some remote location, gifting them pretend marriages only to murder them when their usefulness expired.

Somehow, I know with bone-deep certainty that their bodies number in the dozens, just as I know that it'll be by his hand that I die, not Henry's or Genevieve's. He's the cleaner, the one who makes the messes disappear. Something about that realization sparks a defiance in me that wasn't there before.

I lift my chin, meeting his gaze directly now. If I'm going to die, I won't go as the naive, trusting librarian who stumbled blindly into Eden's web. I'll go as the woman who saw through their lies, who understood the game too late but refused to play by their rules in the end.

His eyes narrow slightly at my changed demeanor, the shift subtle but unmistakable. For a brief moment, I see something flicker across his face—not quite concern, but a recalculation. Like I've become a variable he didn't account for.

"Is something wrong, Morgan?" he asks, his voice gentle but probing.

I offer him a smile that doesn't reach my eyes. "Just processing everything. It's been quite a journey."

His hand comes to rest on my shoulder, the weight of it making my skin crawl. "You've been an exceptional participant in our program. Truly remarkable. Henry has experienced tremendous growth because of you."

"I'm sure he has," I reply, unable to keep the edge from my voice.

Dexter's fingers tighten imperceptibly on my shoulder. "Dr. Warren mentioned the last session was... distressing. Are you alright?"

I turn to face him fully now, slipping from his grasp. "Did she? I suppose I was just emotional about everything that's happened. First time seeing a body, you know?"

His eyes scan my face, looking for cracks in my facade. The practiced smile remains, but I can see the calculation happening behind it. He's assessing risk, determining threat levels. I've become a problem to solve.

"Have I told you that the ceremony will take place by the cliffside?" he asks, changing tactics. "It's one of our most spectacular locations—the ocean stretching out to infinity, the moon lighting it all. A perfect setting for renewal."

A perfect setting for disposal, I think. Easy to push someone over the edge. I wonder if that's how they'll do me in.

"Sounds lovely," I manage.

He checks his watch with deliberate casualness. "We should head there soon. Henry will likely be there already, waiting for us."

"I'd like a moment alone first," I say. "To collect myself."

Something dark passes behind his eyes, there and gone in an instant. "Of course. I'll wait outside."

He moves toward the door, each step measured and controlled. At the threshold, he pauses, turning back to me. "Morgan?"

"Yes?"

"I truly hope you'll embrace this moment. It's the culmination of something extraordinary."

The threat beneath his words is velvet-wrapped and unmistakable. Play your part. Don't make this difficult.

After he closes the door, I exhale shakily, gripping the edge of the vanity to steady myself. My reflection stares back at me—a woman I barely recognize anymore. There's a hollowness in my eyes that wasn't there when I arrived at Eden, but also a hardness that's entirely new.

I think of my life before all this. The quiet library. The lonely apartment. The desperate wish to be chosen, to be loved. How pathetic it all seems now. How shallow my understanding of both love and danger had been.

I should've seen the warning signs. The strange polygraph interview... nobody does that. Why would I have believed Dexter's lies?

Because I was desperate.

But there were others too. Like how they put me, a regular nobody, on a private jet so that there wouldn't be a public record of travel. Or how they took my phone whenever I arrived, so that I couldn't call or message anybody.

I hate that I'd been so foolish, so *blind* to everything.

Well, now I was going to pay the consequences of that. With a heavy sigh, I smooth down my dress, tuck a strand of hair behind my ear—small, meaningless gestures of preparing oneself for the inevitable. If these are to be my final hours, I want to face them with dignity. No begging. No screaming. I'll deny them the satisfaction of my fear.

Maybe death won't be so bad. Maybe there really is peace waiting on the other side.

I pick up the small bouquet of white lilies they've prepared for me—funeral flowers masquerading as wedding blossoms. Fitting, in a macabre way.

When I open the door, Dexter is waiting next to the sleek car I'd seen when I first arrived, his posture relaxed but his eyes vigilant. "Ready?"

I nod, ignoring his offered hand and taking my seat. He circles the vehicle and motions for the driver to drive.

We ride in silence through the resort's manicured grounds. It was for the most part empty, with most of the couples having retired to their suites. The path begins to slope upward as we near the cliffs. The sound of waves crashing against rocks grows louder, nature's own funeral dirge. Salt-laced air fills my lungs, and I breathe deep. It tastes like freedom, in a way—the last pure thing I might experience.

"It's just up ahead," Dexter says, gesturing to a wooden archway wrapped in flowers. Beyond it, I can see the cliff edge, the ceremony site arranged to showcase the spectacular view. White chairs in neat rows. A trellis festooned with tropical blossoms. Everything picture-perfect.

The car stops a short distance away, and Dexter gets out to open my door. But I open it before he can get there, stepping out for myself.

Dexter watches me with growing concern as I take it all in. My calmness must be unsettling to him. By now, most Stand-Ins would be caught up in the romance of it all, or perhaps starting to sense something wrong but unable to name it. I'm doing neither, and it's disrupting his script.

"Before we go any further," he says, stopping me with a gentle touch to my elbow, "I want to assure you that this transition will be handled with the utmost care. You won't experience any discomfort."

The blatant lie almost makes me laugh. He's trying to soothe what he perceives as pre-ceremonial jitters, completely unaware that I know exactly what kind of "transition" awaits me.

"That's very considerate," I reply, my voice steady despite the thunder of my heart.

His eyes search mine, looking for reassurance that I'm still playing along. I give him nothing.

"Morgan," he says, his voice dropping lower, "it's important that you're in the right frame of mind for this. Henry needs to see you happy. Willing. It's crucial for his emotional closure."

Emotional closure. What a delicate way to describe witnessing one's wife being replaced by another.

"I understand," I say, meeting his gaze without flinching. "I know exactly what's expected of me."

Something in my tone must finally penetrate his professional armor, because real concern flashes across his face. "What do you mean by that?"

I smile, a genuine smile this time, because in this moment of clarity, I've found a strange sort of peace. "I mean I'm ready for whatever comes next, Dexter. Ready for the rest of my life."

He stares at me for a long moment, clearly unsettled but unable to articulate why. I can see him wrestling with whether to press further or proceed as planned. The schedule wins out.

"Let's continue then," he says finally, gesturing toward the archway.

I step past him onto the cliff path. The view is breathtaking—endless blue ocean meeting equally vast sky, the sun beginning its descent toward the horizon. Wind whips at my dress and hair, as if nature itself is trying to pull me away from the edge, away from what awaits me.

But I keep walking. One foot in front of the other. Toward the ceremony. Toward the grave.

Behind me, I can feel Dexter's watchful gaze boring into my back.

I can sense his worry.

My smile widens.

THIRTY-EIGHT
HENRY

My jaw clenches, the muscles ticking as my brow furrows deeper with each passing minute. I should already be there, waiting for my real wife to arrive. Instead, I'm stuck here, watching an incompetent driver fumble under the hood of what's meant to be a luxury vehicle.

I sigh and rub my thumb and forefinger against my temple, fighting for patience. The driver has already wasted fifteen minutes with his head buried beneath the hood, muttering to himself. This was meant to be a program of the highest quality—from the resort itself to the resources designed to help me "rediscover what it means to love." And for that promise, I paid top dollar. Well, technically Genevieve paid, though it's my money. She's the one who managed to find Eden in the first place.

And now here I am, stranded on the side of the road like some common tourist.

"Driver, can you please arrange for another transport?" I call out, not bothering to mask the frustration in my voice.

He emerges briefly from under the hood, oil smudged across his forehead. "Of course, Mr. Langford. They are coming."

Right. They're supposedly on their way, though he hasn't made a single call. I let out a slow hiss between my teeth. Why doesn't Eden at least allow their staff phones on this island? The useless landlines in each suite that connect only to reception hardly count as communication.

The car suddenly rumbles to life, and the hood slams shut, revealing the driver's face split with a broad, relieved smile. He quickly jumps back into the driver's seat, adjusting his cap.

"No need to wait anymore, Mr. Langford. I've fixed the situation, and we shall have you there in but a moment."

He steps on the gas, and the car whines as it crawls forward. These sleek vehicles might work well on the resort's flat terrain, but they're useless for speed, let alone climbing the steep path to the cliffside.

The minutes tick by with excruciating slowness. The path winds upward, revealing glimpses of the ocean between lush tropical foliage. The moon hangs high overhead, casting everything in an ethereal white light.

Finally, the car rounds a bend, and there it is—the ceremony site. My breath catches at the sight of Morgan standing at the altar, a bouquet of white lilies in her hands, her face composed as she stares out over the darkening ocean. The white dress she wears seems to capture what little light remains, giving her an almost angelic glow against the backdrop of sea and sky.

She's just as beautiful as the day I first saw her, perhaps even more so in this moment of stillness. I know then, with absolute certainty, that signing the Eden contract was the best decision I ever made.

My gaze drifts to the other figure standing nearby. Dexter, in his perfectly tailored suit that seems fabricated from the night sky itself. He stands with his hands folded in front of him, the picture of professional composure. But something seems off. His normally passive face is tense, his posture too rigid even for him.

Perhaps he's worried about how this vow renewal ceremony will go. The culmination of all Eden's careful work.

He doesn't need to worry, though. I know exactly what needs to be done, and I'm more than happy to do it.

I step out of the car before it fully stops, eager to join Morgan at the altar. To finish what we started. To complete the program.

As I approach, Morgan turns to face me. Something in her eyes gives me pause—a clarity, a sharpness I haven't seen before. Almost as if she's seeing me—truly seeing me—for the first time.

It's probably just nerves, I tell myself. After all, it's a big night for both of us.

The biggest.

Morgan's lips press into a thin line as the wind picks up, whipping tendrils of her hair across her face. The moonlight casts half her features in shadow, the other half glowing with soft light. She's breathtaking—and transparently impatient.

"Let's just start," she says, her voice carrying the slightest edge. "Get this over with."

Dexter steps forward, opening his mouth to speak, but I raise my hand to cut him off.

"We're waiting for someone," I say, offering Morgan a smile I hope seems reassuring. Her eyes narrow. I wonder if she thinks I'm stalling. But she has no idea what's coming.

The minutes stretch uncomfortably. The night grows deeper, clouds shifting slowly overhead. I stare up at the star-studded sky overhead, my hands clammy for some reason.

Dexter checks his watch for the third time in as many minutes; his composure is slipping. Something is definitely off. No one at Eden has ever been anything less than impeccably punctual.

I start to ask what's happening when the soft crunch of tires on gravel announces another arrival.

A silver-haired man in a pressed linen suit emerges from a sleek black car. He looks vaguely familiar—one of Eden's senior staff members, perhaps. He approaches with brisk steps, but his expression is apologetic.

"Mr. and Mrs. Langford, please accept my sincerest apologies for the delay." His voice has that practiced smoothness of someone well-versed in placating wealthy clients. "We're experiencing some... issues with transportation this evening."

I glance over his shoulder at the private airstrip visible in the distance, where the outline of a small plane sits silhouetted against the night sky. I'm guessing he wasn't talking about the plane. He was probably talking about Genevieve. She was supposed to be here by now.

The silver-haired man exchanges a quick glance with Dexter.

"Let's proceed with this particular... portion of the ceremony, shall we?" Dexter asks, though it's not a question.

I look at Dexter. I suppose he thinks that Genevieve being here isn't required just yet. After all, this is about Morgan and me completing this phase of the program. I'm sure Genevieve will make her entrance at the appropriate moment, once I've fulfilled my end of the Eden contract. Once I've shown that I've learned what it means to love again.

"Shall we begin, then?" The silver-haired man gestures toward the altar, strategically positioned at the edge of the cliff to capture the panoramic view of the ocean.

Portable lights flicker on, casting a warm glow as night settles fully around us. The breeze carries the scent of salt and tropical flowers, and somewhere in the distance, waves crash rhythmically against the rocks below.

I take my place opposite Morgan. Up close, I can see the slight tremor in her hands as she grips the lilies. The ceremony begins, the silver-haired man's voice rising and falling with practiced cadence. The words over me—promises of renewal, of rediscovery, of second chances.

I fix my gaze on Morgan's face. She's looking at me,

but there's a vacancy in her expression. Her eyes, usually so expressive, seem hollow.

Numb.

Like she's retreated somewhere deep inside herself, leaving only this beautiful shell standing before me.

The vow man's voice cuts through my observations. "...and now, as we conclude this journey of rediscovery, I ask if either of you would like to speak from the heart." He turns to me. "Mr. Langford? Is there anything you would like to say to Morgan?"

This is it. The moment Eden has been preparing me for.

"Yes," I say, my voice steady despite the sudden pounding of my heart. I don't know why I'm so nervous. There was nothing to be nervous about. My mouth works, like it was expecting a cigarette any moment. I crave it badly, but I force the need down. This isn't the time.

I clear my throat, "There is something I want to say."

Morgan's eyes focus then, sharp and present in a way they haven't been all evening.

And it's then that I see it.

She knows.

I swallow, a bead of sweat rolling down my temple. I take her hands in mine. They're cold despite the humid evening air.

"Morgan," I begin, tasting her name on my lips, savoring it. "I need to thank you."

Something shifts in her expression—a flicker of what looks like... disappointment. Wait, no, is that anger?

My throat bobs as I swallow, and I force myself to continue. "Thank you for the role you've played in my life, for helping me rediscover what it means to love. For reminding me that I'm capable of *feeling* again."

I pause, feeling tears start to well up. At first, I feel shame; my father always said men shouldn't cry. But then, I push that aside, knowing that this moment wasn't like any other. This was me letting go of a part of my life that I would always remember. And that it was *okay* to cry.

"You've given me a gift I can never repay," I say softly. "You've helped me remember who I am, who I was before..." I trail off, leaving the rest unspoken. Before Genevieve. Before our marriage became a war of attrition. Before I became a hollowed-out version of myself.

The sound of another car approaching interrupts my speech. The soft purr of an engine, tires on gravel.

Eve.

My tears dry up at the sight of her stepping out of the car.

Something is wrong.

Terribly, undeniably wrong.

Her normally immaculate appearance is in disarray. Her designer dress is wrinkled, her hair wild and uncombed. But it's her face that sends a chill down my spine—eyes too wide, lips stretched in a smile that borders on rictus. She looks... unhinged.

And then I see what she's carrying.

"Eve?" My voice is barely more than a whisper. "What are you doing?"

She doesn't answer. Her gaze flicks between Morgan and me, then lands on the silver-haired man.

Without warning, she raises the gun and fires.

THIRTY-NINE

MORGAN

Blood splatters across my face, painting it red.

For a surreal moment, no one moves as the deafening gunshot echoes through the silence.

Then the silver-haired man crumples. Numb, I stare at him as the metallic scent of blood fills my nostrils. I can taste the iron, and suddenly, fear washes the numbness away.

All I feel is horror.

She's got a gun.

Henry shouts, stumbling back as reality crashes over us like a tidal wave. "Eve, what have you—"

She turns the gun on him, silencing him.

"You are *so* ungrateful," she hisses, her voice unnaturally calm despite the madness in her eyes. "After everything I've done for you."

"Genevieve, please," he says, raising his hands placatingly.

I look from him to Dexter, who's gone pale. He looks at me, and covered in blood, I smile at him. Fury flashes in his eyes, and he takes a menacing step in my direction, but Genevieve swings the gun in his direction.

"Stop right there!"

Dexter freezes, his gaze still locked onto mine.

"Eve, let's talk about this," Henry says.

"Talk?" She laughs, the sound brittle and sharp enough to cut. She steps closer, swinging the gun back toward him.

I don't bother moving, don't bother making an escape. Because I know I'm going to die here. I'd already accepted that before I stepped up to this altar. There was no escape for me.

But at least Henry and Dexter would meet the same grim end.

"We spent a fortune on this program," she says, her voice rising. "To fix you. To make you love me again. And what do I get? I get to watch you fall in love with *her*." She jerks the gun toward me.

"No, that's not—" he begins, but Genevieve cuts him off with a brittle laugh.

"Don't lie to me. I've been watching you. Both of you." Her eyes are feverish, darting between us. "Did you think I wouldn't know? That I wouldn't see?"

She takes another step forward. Henry takes one back, unaware of how close the cliff edge is behind him.

"Eve, you're not well," he says, struggling to keep his voice steady. "Please, put the gun down. We can get you help."

Something dangerous flashes in her eyes. "Help? Like the 'help' you've been getting? Learning how to love again—just not with me."

"'That's not true," he insists. "Please, I'm here for you."

Genevieve hesitates, like she believes him. The gun lowers a fraction, leaving me wondering if he's *actually* going to talk her out of it. But then he glances toward Dexter and toward me.

Genevieve's eyes harden.

She raises the gun, finger tightening on the trigger. My eyes widen; his gaze snaps back to her.

"No, Eve, don't—"

The second shot feels louder than the first. I feel it before I hear it—the shockwave of pressure as the bullet slams into him, spinning Henry halfway around.

And he topples right over the edge.

FORTY

MORGAN

Time stops.

For one endless moment, I stare at the empty space where Henry had been standing. My brain refuses to process what my eyes have just witnessed—a man, alive one second, gone the next. Not even a scream. Just... absence.

Henry is dead.

The thought hits with physical force, nearly buckling my knees. I expected to feel nothing. Maybe relief. Maybe vindication. But instead, my heart twists with a pain so sharp it steals my breath. A wave of grief hits me, sudden and violent, and I hate myself for it. I hate that I can feel anything for a man who was complicit in my planned murder. A man who'd spent weeks manipulating me, lying to me, all while knowing how this would end.

But I do feel it. God help me, I do.

Genevieve's hollow laughter shatters the moment. Her face is twisted in a grotesque mask of triumph and madness as she stares at the cliff edge.

"He's gone," she whispers, almost wonderingly. "He's really gone."

I take a step back, the movement catching her attention. Her wild eyes lock onto mine.

"And now it's your turn, little stand-in."

Before she can aim, Dexter moves with startling speed. He lunges forward, throwing himself at Genevieve, reaching for the gun. His professionalism has vanished, replaced by desperation.

The gun discharges with a deafening crack. I feel something hot tear through my thigh, and the world tilts sideways as my leg buckles beneath me.

I scream, the sound raw and primal, as I collapse to the ground. Blood pours between my fingers as I clutch at the wound. Pain lances through me, white-hot and clarifying. And with it comes a realization...

I don't want to die.

Not here. Not now. Not like this.

The struggle continues mere feet away from me—Dexter and Genevieve locked in struggle, the gun between them, their faces contorted with effort. I drag my eyes from them to the airstrip in the distance, where the silhouette of the plane sits dark against the night sky.

A chance. Just a small chance.

But I've already accepted death once tonight. I accepted it when I walked up here in this white dress, when I stood at this altar and looked into the eyes of the man who used me and made me temporary. I accepted it because I had no choice.

But now? Now there might be another option. If I can just get to that plane...

Without conscious thought, I drag myself forward, teeth gritted against the agony in my leg. Blood trails behind me, marking my path across the pristine white altar cloth. I reach for one of the decorative metal stands holding the lanterns, wrapping my fingers around its cold surface.

A weapon. It's not much of one, but it's something.

I haul myself upright and limp toward the struggle, the stand clutched in trembling hands. Genevieve has pushed Dexter back, the gun wavering between them as they circle each other.

Neither notices me approaching.

"I don't know what you're doing," Dexter spits at Genevieve. "Everything was on track. He was going to renew his vow with you!"

"His vow?" Genevieve laughs, the sound unhinged. "You have no idea."

I'm close enough now. Close enough to swing.

But as I raise the metal stand, Genevieve is shoved hard enough to send her falling backward. She lands with a heavy grunt, and the gun skitters across the ground, coming to rest at my feet. Our eyes meet. For one frozen moment, we both stare at the weapon.

Then we lunge.

My fingers close around the cold metal first. I spin around, ignoring the screaming pain in my leg, and aim the gun as she advances on me. Her momentum carries her forward even as recognition dawns in her eyes.

I pull the trigger.

The recoil jolts up my arm as the gun discharges.

Genevieve's forehead erupts in a spray of red. Her body crumples like a marionette with cut strings, folding in on itself before hitting the ground with a sickening thud.

I stand there, panting, smoke curling from the barrel. My hands are shaking so violently I can barely maintain my grip. Did I just—? Did I really just—?

"Well," Dexter's cool voice cuts through my shock. "I severely underestimated you, Morgan."

I swing the gun toward him, forcing my hands to steady. He stands a few feet away, his perfect suit spattered with blood, his expression unnervingly calm despite the carnage surrounding us.

"Don't move," I warn, my voice hoarse.

He raises an eyebrow, unmoved by the weapon pointed at his chest. "What exactly is your plan here? Shoot me and what? Take the pilot hostage and fly away?"

I ground my teeth, because that was *exactly* my plan.

He gives me that same professional smile that disarmed me the first day I'd met him. "Where would you go? Who would believe your story?"

"Shut up," I hiss, taking a limping step toward him. "You're coming with me. You're going to get me that pilot, and I'm going to get off this island."

His smile widens, and his usual professional mask slips. In its place is something genuine, and far more terrifying. "Oh, Morgan. You have no idea what you're up against. Eden has money, power, resources. They won't let you get away with this. You have no home to shelter in, nobody to turn to."

"You think I care?" I laugh, even as my finger tightens on the trigger. I could do it. I could pull the trigger right now and end whatever threat he's posing. I've already killed once tonight. What's one more? "It's *because* of all that that I'll be free. You won't find me. Not when I could be anywhere. Bali, Algeria, Madagascar, wherever I want to go, I'll go. And you won't even know."

"Hiding takes money, librarian. Something *you* don't have."

"You think so?"

He hesitates.

"You're so stupid. You think I didn't get Henry's bank details before all of this?" I lie, knowing that it means nothing. But the lie tastes so good, and even better when his smile devolves into an ugly snarl.

"Into the driver seat. You do as I say, I'll let you live. I'll promise you that much."

He pauses.

"Get moving!"

His eyes hold mine, calculating, measuring. Then he shrugs, as if my holding a gun on him is merely an inconvenience. "As you wish."

We climb into Genevieve's car, and I press the gun to the back of his headrest, my finger itching to pull the trigger. He slowly drives me toward the airstrip, leaving behind three bodies cooling in the night air.

I glance down at the blood soaking the pristine white of my dress. I wonder if anybody else on the resort heard the gunshots. If so, what would they think?

Somehow, I doubted that they'd see it for what it was.

After all, the idea of gunshots ringing out on the Eden island of paradise? Unthinkable.

I don't look back at Henry's absence, at the cliff edge where he vanished. I can't afford to. Not now.

But as I ride, his final expression haunts me. And beneath the fear and adrenaline, beneath the desperate will to survive, I feel that twist in my heart again.

That grief I shouldn't feel.

The car lurches to a stop at the edge of the airstrip. The small private jet sits on the tarmac, its white body gleaming under the moonlight. A pair of ground staff in Eden uniforms are refueling it, and they turn at our arrival, their expressions shifting from professional politeness to confusion as they take in the blood-soaked state of my dress.

"Stay in the car," I tell Dexter, pressing the gun harder against his headrest. "Call them over."

He hesitates, then rolls down his window. "We need immediate departure," he calls out, his voice regaining some of its usual authoritative tone. "Prepare the aircraft."

One of the ground crew approaches, his eyes widening as he gets close enough to see my state and the gun in my hand.

"Mr. Dexter, what's—"

"There's been an incident," Dexter cuts him off smoothly. "An incident requiring medical attention on the mainland."

The man looks unconvinced, his gaze flicking between us. "Sir, protocol states—"

"To hell with protocol," I snap, leaning forward so he can see me clearly. "Get the pilot. Now."

He takes a step back, hand moving to his belt where a radio is clipped. "I need to call this in."

"No!" I thrust the gun forward, and he freezes. "No calls. No radio. Just get the pilot."

His partner has noticed the commotion and approaches cautiously. I can see the exact moment he registers the situation—his body stiffening, eyes darting to his colleague's for confirmation that this is really happening.

"Both of you, back away from the plane," I order, my voice steadier than I feel. "Dexter, get out. Slowly."

Dexter hesitates, but with one wave of the gun, he obeys.

Blood has soaked through the bandage I hastily fashioned from a torn strip of my dress, and the pain is getting harder to ignore. I need to be on that plane and out of here *now*, before I lost my strength and energy and these men took advantage of that.

More lights have come on around the resort. Someone must have heard the gunshots after all. In the distance, I can see figures moving, heading in our direction.

Dexter looks toward them and smiles, a hint of satisfaction in his voice. "This ends here, Morgan."

"Shut up and move toward the plane."

We make our way across the tarmac, me limping behind him with the gun pressed to his back. The ground crew back away, hands raised.

"Tell them to stay back," I order, as more Eden staff emerge from the path to the resort.

"Everyone stay where you are!" he calls out, and to

my surprise, they obey, stopping at the edge of the airstrip. Maybe they think he has the situation under control. Maybe they're just waiting for an opportunity.

The plane's door opens, and a pilot appears at the top of the stairs, taking in the scene with professional calm.

"We need to leave. Now," I tell him, gesturing with the gun.

His eyes dart to Dexter, looking for confirmation.

"Do as she says," Dexter says through gritted teeth, and the pilot nods once, disappearing back inside to prepare for takeoff.

We climb the stairs, my leg screaming in protest with each step. Inside, the jet is as luxurious as I expected— plush leather seats, polished wood trim, crystal decanters on a small bar. The kind of extravagance that Henry would have been used to.

I'm sure there's a first aid kit somewhere on board. Wouldn't surprise me if they had surgical supplies, even.

I push Dexter into a seat. "Hands where I can see them."

He complies, placing his palms on his knees, watching me with that calculating gaze.

The pilot's voice comes over the intercom. "Please be seated for takeoff. We'll be airborne in two minutes."

Security personnel have reached the edge of the tarmac now, a dozen of them forming a loose semicircle around the plane. One steps forward, speaking into a megaphone.

"This is Eden Security. Step out of the aircraft immediately."

I laugh, though it comes out as more of a sob. "No way."

The engines whine to life, drowning out further commands from outside. I strap myself in across from Dexter, keeping the gun trained on him as the plane begins to taxi. Through the window, I can see the security team's frustration, their helpless gestures as they realize they can't stop what's happening.

The jet picks up speed, racing down the runway, and then we're airborne, the island falling away beneath us. Only when we've reached cruising altitude, the seat belt sign dimming, do I allow myself to exhale.

I was actually escaping.

I turn my attention back to Dexter, finally asking the question that's been burning inside me since I discovered the truth. "Why?"

He studies me for a long moment, as if deciding whether answering is worth his time.

Finally, he shrugs. "Money. Power. Favors... It turns out that when you save a person's marriage, they're happy to be indebted to you."

I stare at him, disbelieving of how easy he found all of this: manipulating people, using them and discarding them when their purpose was served.

"How do you sleep at night?"

"Like a baby," he replies, then his expression shifts, becoming almost sympathetic. "You're not special, Morgan. You're not the first to discover the truth, though you're certainly the first to get this far. I commend you for that."

"I don't want your commendation," I spit.

"What do you want, then? Money? I can arrange it. A new identity? Eden has resources. Perhaps we can come to an arrangement."

I stare at him, stunned by his audacity. "You think I would work with you? After everything?"

"I think you're practical. I think you want to live." He leans back, confident again. "Without Eden's protection, you won't last a month. To the outside world, you'll be the one who killed Henry and Genevieve Langford, one of the wealthiest families in the country. Their families will want answers. The authorities will be looking for you. You're a librarian from nowhere with no resources, no connections."

He's right, and we both know it. But there's something he doesn't understand.

"I'd rather die than become like you," I tell him, and I mean it.

"Noble," he says with a patronizing smile. "But ultimately foolish."

The pilot's voice crackles over the intercom. "Mr. Dexter, we'll need a destination soon."

Dexter raises an eyebrow. "Well? Where shall we go? Keep in mind, Eden has connections everywhere. There's nowhere you can hide that we won't find you."

I look out the window, eyes locked onto the distant resort shrinking in the distance. For some reason, I remember an off-hand comment Henry made about a small coastal town in Portugal with a cliff-side cafe that he loved. He'd only ever been there by himself, when he felt lonely.

What was it called?

Cascais.

That's right.

I glance back just in time to catch the sudden movement of his hand.

My finger squeezes the trigger.

The sound is deafening in the confined space of the cabin. Dexter jerks backward, a look of surprise crossing his face as red blooms across his crisp white shirt. He stares at me for one long moment, then slumps forward.

The pilot's voice crackles over the intercom, panicked. "What was that? What's happening?"

"Everything's under control," I call back, my voice steadier than I expected.

I force myself to my feet, every step a reminder of the pain, the blood loss, the sheer exhaustion pressing in. But I keep moving, dragging myself toward the cockpit, the gun hanging loose at my side.

"Portugal," I say, leaning against the doorframe. "Will that be a problem?"

The pilot pales, his gaze flicking to the weapon. He swallows hard. Shakes his head.

"Good. And do you know how to keep a secret?"

A quick, desperate nod. He's seen the blood. The way I carry myself now—lighter. Dangerous. It's one thing to see someone hold a gun. It's another to know they've already used it.

"Do you work for Eden?"

He exhales shakily. "No. I'm contracted. Private charter service."

I gesture to the dash. "Are they tracking us?"

"I can turn it off."

"Then do that." My voice is quiet, firm. "And I'll let you live. My problem's not with you. We have a deal?"

A beat. Then he breathes out, a mix of relief and fear. "Yes, ma'am."

I watch as he flicks a series of switches, cutting the signal. The soft beeping vanishes. For the first time since boarding this plane, I exhale.

I turn, staggering back to my seat. The gun is still in my grip, but my fingers are numb now, the weight of everything pressing in. The adrenaline that kept me moving is draining fast, leaving me lightheaded, trembling.

I glance down at my dress.

White, ruined. A vow renewal dress turned funeral shroud.

A slow, shuddering breath escapes me as I press my forehead against the cool glass of the window. Below, the ocean stretches endlessly, its dark surface smooth, unbothered. As if none of it—the blood, the bodies, the betrayals—ever happened.

I close my eyes.

And I see them all: Brody, Luka, the silver-haired man conducting the vow renewal ceremony, Genevieve, even Dexter.

And of course... Henry.

I open my eyes, and look down at the diamond ring on my finger. I should take it off, flush it down the toilet. But for some reason, I don't.

Maybe it's because I know it'll sell for a good amount, enough to get me settled for a bit. Maybe it's because I'm still here, despite everything.

Or maybe, just maybe, it's because there's a part of me that will always love him.

I push the thought away and stare into the open sky. The island shrinks into nothing, swallowed by the horizon. And allowing myself a smile, I finally let Eden disappear.

FORTY-ONE

EDEN

I scroll through the images on my tablet, the soft glow illuminating my face as I sit in my office on the ninety-third floor of our Manhattan headquarters. Outside the floor-to-ceiling windows, the city sprawls like a living thing, its lights twinkling in the gathering dusk.

First, I look at Eden as it was meant to be seen—aerial shots of our pristine resort, white sand beaches, and lush tropical foliage. Then I tap the screen, and the images change. Now there are crime scene photos. Blood on white altar cloth. Outlines where bodies were found. A cliff edge, roped off with yellow tape.

"Tell me again," I say, keeping my voice as smooth and cold as the polished black marble beneath my fingertips.

Katherine shifts her weight slightly, the only outward sign of her discomfort. Her navy suit is impeccably tailored, her hair pulled into a severe bun. She could be mistaken for a high-powered attorney or corporate executive. In a way, she is both for Eden.

"The situation devolved rapidly," she begins.

"Genevieve Langford shot her husband, and he fell over the cliff edge. He survived the fall, but barely. He's currently in critical condition at our private medical facility in Zurich."

I lift my eyebrows slightly. "What is the prognosis?"

"Uncertain. Multiple fractures, internal bleeding, severe head trauma. The doctors are skeptical about his chances, but they haven't ruled out recovery."

"I see. And Genevieve Langford?"

"Dead. Shot by the Stand-In Wife, who then killed Dexter as well and commandeered the private jet. We've lost contact with the aircraft."

I pinch the bridge of my nose, the first sign of emotion I've allowed myself to show. "And the pilot?"

"Contracted through our usual service. Not Eden personnel."

"So, to summarize," I say, placing the tablet facedown on the desk, "we've lost one high-profile client, our best Match Coordinator and several staff, another client is hanging by a thread, and we've allowed a witness to escape. Is that an accurate assessment of this cata-strophe?"

Katherine doesn't flinch. "Yes, sir."

I stare at her a moment longer, then sigh. "And the Stand-In Wife? Morgan, was it?"

"We're monitoring all ports of entry, and we've flagged her identity with our contacts. So far, nothing."

"What about the aircraft?"

"No location. The transponder went dark."

I nod slowly, as if this information merely confirms

what I already suspected. "And you believe she's still alive?"

"It's... possible."

My mouth twists into something almost resembling a smile. "A librarian from nowhere. No special training, no resources, no connections. And yet, she managed to cause all this." I tap my fingers against the marble. "Impressive."

"Should we allocate additional resources to find her, sir? I can have a team—"

I wave her off. "No. For now, passive monitoring only. If she surfaces and starts talking, then we can eliminate the problem. Otherwise..." I trail off, making a dismissive gesture. "No point throwing good money after bad."

"And Langford? If he survives?"

"He's under contract. The NDAs he signed are watertight." I lean back in my chair, considering. "Still, we should ensure he has everything he needs. If there's anything he wants—specialists, experimental treatments, comfort measures—give it to him."

"Sir?"

"It's important that we maintain good relationships with customers we've failed, especially ones as wealthy and well-connected as Henry Langford." I offer her a thin smile. "Besides, a satisfied customer, even a damaged one, is less likely to pursue other... avenues of redress."

"Understood."

"In the meantime, liquidate the island operation. Sell off the assets. Make sure anyone who might have witnessed anything problematic is reassigned to more discrete positions."

The euphemism hangs in the air between us. We both know what "reassigned" really means.

"It's imperative that we maintain our reputation," I continue, turning to look out at the city below. "Eden provides a valuable service to those who can afford it. One unfortunate incident doesn't change that."

"Of course, sir."

"And the other therapy programs?"

"Proceeding according to plan. We have three vow renewals scheduled this month."

I nod, satisfied. "Good. Focus on those. Eden is bigger than one island, after all. The work continues."

Katherine inclines her head in agreement. "Is there anything else, sir?"

I consider for a moment. "Have Accounting prepare a full financial assessment of the damages. Have Legal prepare our standard containment protocols, in case they're needed. And keep me updated on Langford's condition."

"Right away, sir."

She turns to leave, her heels clicking sharply on the polished floor. As the door closes behind her, I pick up the tablet again, swiping through the crime scene photos one more time.

My lips twitch in something close to admiration.

"Well played, librarian," I murmur to the empty room. "Well played."

With a flick of my finger, I delete the photos. Time to move on. Time to move on. The world is full of wealthy people with marriage problems, and Eden will continue to offer the best therapy money can buy.

For the right price.

FORTY-TWO

HENRY

I'm falling.

Time slows to a crawl. Morgan's face twists in horror; Eve's shifts from rage to some sick satisfaction. I see the night sky, stars wheeling above me as I tumble over the cliff's edge.

And then there's nothing but the rush of wind in my ears and the certainty of the rocks below.

All those weeks of therapy, of carefully facilitated "growth"—they weren't about saving my marriage at all. It was about learning to feel again, yes, but not for Genevieve's benefit.

For mine.

The wind rushes past, and I wait for the impact that will end it all. My last thought is of Morgan's face—not as she looked that night under the moonlight, remote and numb, but as she looked when I carried her in my arms up that slope that first day we married: laughing, sunlight in her hair, truly alive in a way I haven't been for years.

The irony isn't lost on me. I finally remembered how to love, just in time to die.

The darkness rushes up to meet me, and—

I gasp and jolt awake.

Pain. That's the first thing I register. Not the dull, distant ache of a hangover or the sharp twinge of a pulled muscle. This is something else entirely—a symphony of agony playing through every inch of my body. My ribs scream. My head pounds. Even breathing feels like swallowing fire.

White ceiling. Unfamiliar. Sterile. A rhythmic beeping keeps time with my heartbeat. Antiseptic stings my nostrils.

Hospital. I'm in a hospital.

Which means I'm still *alive*.

I try to move and instantly regret it, a groan escaping my cracked lips. A figure in a white coat materializes beside me.

"Mr. Langford, please remain still. You've suffered extensive injuries."

The doctor is a woman in her fifties, with silver-streaked hair pulled back in a practical ponytail. Her accent is vaguely Germanic. Swiss, maybe. Her expression is professionally neutral as she checks the monitors beside my bed.

"Where—" My voice cracks, my throat as dry as sandpaper.

"You're in a private medical facility in Zurich," she answers. "You've been unconscious for eight days. You're lucky to be alive."

Lucky isn't the word I'd choose. The memories come

flooding back in jagged fragments. The ceremony. The shot. Genevieve. The fall.

Morgan.

"My wife," I manage to croak. "Where is she?"

The doctor exchanges a glance with someone I hadn't noticed—a man in a dark suit by the door.

Eden.

"I'm afraid Mrs. Langford didn't survive," the man says.

For a moment, I don't react. I stare at the ceiling, searching for the grief I should be feeling. My wife of five years is dead. I should be devastated. Instead, I feel...nothing.

No, that's not quite right.

I feel relief. A terrible, guilty relief.

Because she wasn't the one I was asking about.

"Not her," I whisper, my voice gaining strength. "The other one. Where is she?"

The man blinks, surprised.

"Mr. Langford," the doctor begins cautiously, "you've suffered a severe head trauma. Some confusion is to be expected—"

"I'm not confused," I cut her off, ignoring the pain that flares with each word. "Morgan. Where is Morgan?"

"Perhaps this discussion should wait until you're stronger," the doctor suggests.

I try to sit up, ignoring the explosion of pain in my chest. "Tell me."

"I—"

"I wasn't speaking to you." I level the doctor with a

stare, then turn to the man from Eden. "I was speaking to *you*."

A beat passes. Then he steps forward. "Ms. Sloane left the island. We're not sure where she is."

Left. *She got away.* Relief floods through me, stronger than the pain.

"Eden would like to assure you that we're doing everything possible to ensure your comfort and recovery," the man adds, his tone shifting to one of careful deference. "If there's anything you need or want, you have only to ask."

Of course. I'm still a client. A valuable one, despite everything. Or perhaps because of everything. A wealthy man who knows too much.

I close my eyes, pretending exhaustion. "I need to rest."

"Of course." The doctor adjusts something in my IV. "This will help with the pain."

Within moments, a warm numbness begins to spread through my veins. But before I let it carry me away, I make a decision.

I'm going to find her.

Not today. Not tomorrow. But as soon as I can stand, as soon as I can walk, I'm going to start looking. The edges of my vision start to blur as the sedative pulls me toward unconsciousness.

But all I can think about is her. She taught me how to feel again. How to care. How to love. And love isn't what I thought it was. It isn't exotic resorts and vow renewals and therapists with hidden agendas.

Real love is messy. It takes work and risk and sacrifice. Real love is choosing someone, over and over, even when it's hard.

Even when it seems impossible.

I'm not sure if she'll have me when I do find her. After all, I signed the contract, content to use her and discard her when I was done. But I love her enough to try and spend the rest of my life making it up to her.

As my consciousness slips away, I dream not of falling, but of flying—soaring over oceans and mountains, following an invisible thread that leads me to her. To the woman who taught me how to live again.

She was always the choice.

My lips part to tell her. To whisper the words I should have said long before.

But the darkness swallows me, leaving just one, final thought lingering.

I still have my vows to finish.

ABOUT THE AUTHOR

Zia Rayyan is a psychological thriller author with no background, no alibi—only a need to write about the lies we tell, and the ones we bury.

You can reach Zia at ziarayyan.com or by email at zia. rayyan.author@gmail.com.

You may also see Zia being quite active in the Psychological Thriller Readers Facebook group—come join the community. But only if you can keep a secret.

Printed in Dunstable, United Kingdom